CLAUDIA AND THE CLUE
IN THE PHOTOGRAPH

"Who's there?" I yelled. There was no answer. I sat there in the dark for a second, holding the reel of film. Then I dumped it into the tank and screwed the lid on. I would still develop it, just in case there were a few pictures that weren't completely ruined. As soon as the film was in the tank, I reached up and turned on the lights. Then I opened the bathroom door and peered out.

"Anybody there?" I called. "Janine? Mum? Dad?" There was no answer. Suddenly, I felt a chill. Who had opened the door? And where was that person now? I had thought I was alone in the house.

Also available in the Babysitters Club Mysteries series:

No 1: Stacey and the Missing Ring
No 2: Beware, Dawn!
No 3: Mallory and the Ghost Cat
No 4: Kristy and the Missing Child
No 5: Mary Anne and the Secret in the Attic
No 6: The Mystery at Claudia's House
No 7: Dawn and the Disappearing Dogs
No 8: Jessi and the Jewel Thieves
No 9: Kristy and the Haunted Mansion
No 10: Stacey and the Mystery Money
No 11: Claudia and the Mystery at the Museum
No 12: Dawn and the Surfer Ghost
No 13: Mary Anne and the Library Mystery
No 14: Stacey and the Mystery at the Mall
No 15: Kristy and the Vampires

Look out for:

No 17: Dawn and the Halloween Mystery
No 18: Stacey and the Mystery of the Empty House
No 19: Kristy and the Missing Fortune

CLAUDIA AND THE CLUE IN THE PHOTOGRAPH

Ann M. Martin

The author gratefully acknowledges
Ellen Miles
for her help in preparing this manuscript.

Scholastic Children's Books,
Commonwealth House, 1–19 New Oxford Street,
London WC1A 1NU, UK
a division of Scholastic Ltd
London ~ New York ~ Toronto ~ Sydney ~ Auckland

First published in the US by Scholastic Inc., 1994
First published in the UK by Scholastic Ltd, 1996

Text copyright © Ann M. Martin, 1994
THE BABYSITTERS CLUB is a registered trademark of Scholastic Inc.

ISBN 0 590 13477 9

Typeset in Plantin by Contour Typesetters, Southall, London
Printed by Cox & Wyman Ltd, Reading, Berks.

10 9 8 7 6 5 4 3 2

1st CHAPTER

"Claudia, *please*!" Janine put down her fork. "I would prefer not to be recorded for posterity in the act of chewing a mouthful of Shredded Wheat."

"It's not for posterity," I said, still peering at my older sister through the viewfinder of the camera, "whatever *that* is. It's for Mr Geist's class." Janine is always using words I don't know, but I don't let it bother me.

"Claudia, please put that camera down and eat your breakfast," said my mother, handing me a plate with two pieces of raisin toast on it.

"But Mum, Mr Geist says we have to learn to 'catch the moment'. It's what all the best photographers do." I turned to focus on *her* through the viewfinder. She looked a little peeved.

"That may be so," said my father. "But

1

the Kishi family at breakfast is one moment you're not going to catch. Besides, you're going to get jam on my camera if you're not careful." He reached out for the camera. I put the lens cap back on and handed it to him. He turned it over in his hands. "What a great piece of equipment," he said. He squinted through the viewfinder. "This Minolta and I go way, way back."

"I know," I said, "and I really appreciate your lending it to me. I've been super-careful with it." I had, too. My dad's old Minolta hasn't got the most up-to-date features, but it *is* a terrific camera. "Mr Geist says it's a classic," I told my dad.

Mr Geist was my photography teacher. He was one of the best teachers I'd ever had at SMS. (That's Stoneybrook Middle School, which is in Stoneybrook, Connecticut, the town where I live.) Taking photography with Mr Geist made going to summer school not just bearable, but really great. At first, when my parents insisted I do maths again this summer, I was really upset. But then we made a deal. If I had to do maths, I would also be allowed to do another course, just for fun. At the time, I didn't know just how *much* fun photography would be. But the fact is that Mr Geist had opened up a new world for me, and now I couldn't think about anything but photography.

You've probably already worked out that my name's Claudia Kishi, and that I've got an older sister called Janine who is incredibly brainy. (She's a genius, in fact.) And you might have guessed that my family is very close, because of the way we were all sitting down to breakfast together. And maybe you've also realized that I can get totally wrapped up in other things like photography. Well, you're right on all counts, especially the last one.

I've loved art for as long as I can remember. Other kids would do a little crayoning and then move on to playing with dolls or riding bikes. Me? I moved from crayoning to finger-painting to papier-mâché and then back to crayoning. For me, there's nothing like the feeling you get from *creating* something, something that's yours alone. And now, this summer, I'd discovered a whole new way to create.

First I'd learned how to use a camera—a *real* camera, not the automatic kind you take snapshots with. And while I hate maths, somehow I had no problem working out exposures and shutter speeds. Then I'd learned about the elements of a good picture. Mr Geist had taught me how to consider composition, textures, forms and tones so that I could produce not

3

just snapshots, but pieces of art that would really have an effect on the viewer. And last of all, I'd learned how to make magic.

That's right, magic.

Have you ever worked in a darkroom? If you have, you know what I'm talking about. If you haven't, you'll just have to take my word for it. What happens in that lightless place is pure magic. I'll never forget the first time I put a plain white piece of paper into a tray of developer and saw the image form itself in front of my eyes. I felt like a wizard!

My dad, who used to do a lot of photography himself, had noticed how excited I was about my class. "Tell you what," he'd said, one night after supper. "How about if we make you a temporary darkroom in the bathroom between your room and Janine's?" He'd rounded up all the equipment—some borrowed, some rented, some bought—and helped me set up my very own wizard's den.

I'd been spending every spare minute in there ever since.

Well, maybe not *every* minute. As always, I'm also spending plenty of time on one of my other loves, babysitting. I belong to this cool club called the BSC, or Babysitters Club. My best pal Stacey McGill is in it, too, and so are a lot of my other good friends. We all have different interests, but one thing we have in common is that we adore kids. That's why the club (it's actually more of a business) works so well. But more about that later.

Back to that Friday morning, when my family kept me from "catching the moment". I'd hardly finished my toast when my mother glanced at her watch and gave a little yelp. "It's late!" she said. "I've got to run." She gave us each a quick kiss and, grabbing an overstuffed briefcase, headed out to her job as head librarian at the Stoneybrook Public Library. Soon after that my dad took off for *his* job, which has something to do with stocks and bonds of money. (I've never quite understood what he does, but apparently he's very good at it.)

Janine took one last sip of juice and picked up her rucksack.

"Ready to crunch those numbers?" I asked, grinning. This summer, Janine had signed up for a work-study programme that's part of this supersonic academic fast track she's on. She's still at high school, but she takes a lot of college classes. For summer school, she was taking what she called a "light" schedule. Light for an Einstein like her, maybe.

Janine's work-study programme involved helping one of her professors with some research. When I first heard that, I thought she might be doing something halfway interesting, like teaching rats how to go through a maze. But no, all she was doing was sitting in front of a computer for hours at a time, typing in numbers. According to Janine, it was "utterly fascinating". I'd rather watch bread get stale, myself.

"I wish you wouldn't use that vulgar expression," said Janine, sniffing. "I'm not 'crunching' *anything*. I'm performing quantitative data analysis."

Yikes! "Whatever," I said. "Have a blast!" I waved goodbye to her, and then ran upstairs for a final outfit-check.

Most people just wear cut-off jeans and T-shirts to summer school. Not me. I consider getting dressed to be as much of a creative act as painting on a canvas or sculpting with clay. I plan my outfits with care, and I make a point of never wearing exactly the same thing twice. Not that I have several wardrobes full of clothes, or anything. It's just that I like to combine what I *do* have in new and interesting ways.

I stood in front of my full-length mirror and looked. Staring back at me was a medium-height Japanese-American girl with almond-shaped eyes and long, black hair held back by a pink, star-shaped hairclip. She was wearing a silky pink tank top with a man's white shirt tied casually over it, white jeans, and flip-flops decorated with more pink stars.

I gave my reflection the thumbs-up sign. "Okay, Kishi, I think you're ready," I said to myself. "Except for one thing." I turned and checked under the pillow on my bed. "Provisions!" I cried, when I'd found what I was looking for. I stuck the Milky Way bar into my rucksack.

I have something to confess. I'm a junk food fiend.

Yes, it's true. You might not be able to tell by looking at me, but I practically *live* on foods containing long lists of ingredients I can't pronounce. Tortilla chips, crisps, corn chips, pretzels, Milky Ways, M&M's, Polos and Twizzlers. I love them, I love them, I love them. But my parents seem to have this bizarre idea that all that stuff is bad for me and that I should be eating carrots and beetroots instead. Right.

To humour my parents, I eat carrots and beetroot at the family table, but I'll never give up my junk food. It's hidden all over my room. I'm never far from a chocolate bar: that's my motto.

My poor misguided parents also disapprove of my habit of reading Nancy Drew books—"junk food for the mind"—as my mother calls them. I keep telling her that if she ever read one of them, she'd understand why I like them so much, but she just shakes her head, smiles and hands me a paperback copy of some impossible-to-read "classic" like *The Scarlet Pimple*, or whatever it's called. I always take the book, stick it on my shelf, and then pull a Nancy Drew mystery from behind my bedside table and read to my heart's content.

Anyway, that morning I had no time for reading of any kind. I had to hurry if I was going to be in my seat by the time my maths teacher, Mr Davies, handed out that day's test.

I won't bore you with the details of my maths class, except to mention that Mr Davies was wearing a gorgeous red tie that looked as though it might have been made of tie-dyed silk. I made a few notes reminding myself to experiment with tie-dyeing fine fabrics, raced through the test, and then headed downstairs to the photo lab.

That day's class with Mr Geist was excellent, as always. The lecture part was about making portraits, and Mr Geist showed us loads of great slides that illustrated the points he was making. Afterwards, we had time to do a little work in the darkroom.

The last bell rang just as we were cleaning up. I raced home, my head full of ideas about how to capture people on film. I had yesterday's roll of film to develop first. It included some fashion shots of Stacey acting like a model, and I couldn't wait to see how they'd turned out.

I walked into the kitchen, thinking hard about my portrait assignment, and nearly bumped into Janine. "What are *you* doing here?" I asked.

"Professor Woodley doesn't need me till two today," she said, "so I came home to have a quick lunch and pick up my notebook."

I made us a couple of grilled cheese sandwiches, and we ate together without talking much. I was still thinking about my new ideas, and Janine was poring over columns of figures in her notebook. She hardly lifted her head when I cleared my plate and told her I would be in the darkroom for a while.

I went up to our bathroom and began to assemble all the things I would need for developing my roll of film. First, I set up my clock radio, tuning into my favourite station and making sure the clock was turned on so that I could see it while the film developed. Keeping track of time is an essential part of working in a darkroom. Then I got out all my chemicals and measuring cups and arranged them, along with my thermometer (the temperature of the chemicals is important, too), my developing tank, my bottle opener (to prise the

9

top off the film canister), and my scissors (to cut off the end of the film).

I know it sounds like a complicated process, but really, developing film is incredibly easy. The most important thing is to have total—and I mean *total*—darkness while you're loading the film into a developing tank. You *can* load film in a lighted room, by using a changing bag, which is a rubberized sack with places to put your hands in. But it's not easy to fumble around in there with the reels and the bottle opener and all that. I'd rather load film in a lightproof room, and my dad and I had made sure that the bathroom, which hasn't got any windows, was as lightproof as possible. All I had to do to make it totally dark was shove a towel into the crack at the bottom of the door and turn off the lights.

Which is what I did. Then, in the pitch-dark, I sat on my stool next to the counter, and felt around for the film and all my equipment. As I had arranged everything so carefully, it only took me a few minutes to get the film out of the can and loaded on to the reel. I had just dropped the reel into the developing tank, knowing that as soon as I put on the lid, the tank would be lightproof and I could turn on the lights, when I heard a tapping at the door.

"Claud?" asked Janine. I heard the door-knob turning.

"No!" I yelled. "Don't come in or—"

Janine pulled the door open and poked her head inside. Light from the hallway flooded into the darkroom. "What did you say?"

"—or you'll ruin my film," I finished, slapping the lid on to the tank as quickly as I could.

Janine put her hand over her mouth. "Oh, no!" she said. "I'm so sorry, Claud! I didn't realize—"

"It's okay," I said, even though I was pretty upset. It was easy to see that Janine felt terrible. "I might be able to salvage the negatives."

Janine apologized about three hundred times more and then, at last, she left. I shut the door behind her, promising myself to make a *Darkroom in Use* sign for it, and looked at the tank. If I was lucky, there might be a few frames on the roll that hadn't been destroyed. Stacey would be coming over that afternoon for our BSC meeting, and if I hurried, I might be able to show her some negatives from our "fashion shoot". I turned up the radio and settled down to work.

2nd CHAPTER

By five-twenty that afternoon, I had not only finished developing the film, but I had also done my maths homework. (Yea, Claud!) The negatives *were* pretty much ruined. There was a grey fog covering almost every shot. With careful work, I might be able to print *parts* of each picture, but the fact was, it would be easier just to shoot the whole roll over again. I knew Stacey wouldn't mind posing for me one more time. She had loved playing model.

I was sitting at my desk, looking over the negatives with an eyeglass (a kind of mini magnifying glass), when I glanced at my clock and realized my friends would start arriving any minute for our BSC meeting. I put the negatives away and picked up my camera. While I was working in the dark-room, I'd been thinking about what Mr

Geist had said about creating portraits, and I'd come up with a great idea. You see, Mr Geist had talked about "capturing the essence" of a person on film. A good picture of somebody shouldn't just show what they *look* like, he said, it should show what they *are* like. So my idea was to take a picture of each of my friends as they entered my room, as an exercise in making portraits.

I would use black-and-white film, so I could develop it myself. Black-and-white is best for portraits, anyway. All the best photographers use it. I couldn't wait to see whether my quick shots would capture my friends' personalities.

Just as I was taking the lens cap off my camera, I heard the front door slam. Then I heard footsteps thumping up the stairs, and I knew by their sound that Kristy Thomas was about to arrive. Quickly, I aimed the camera at the door to my room, focused and set the correct exposure for the amount of light. As I peered through the viewfinder, Kristy appeared, framed by the doorway. "Say cheese!" I called out quickly.

Kristy stopped in her tracks, gave me a huge grin, and shot me the peace sign with both hands. *Snap!*

Perfect. The picture would show what Kristy looks like: short, with dark hair and eyes—they're brown, really—dressed in

13

trainers, jeans and a T-shirt (Kristy's uniform!). But it also *definitely* captured Kristy's essence. Confident, outgoing and full of energy; that's Kristy. She's chairman of the BSC, and with good reason. For one thing, she came up with the idea for the club. And for another, she keeps adding plenty of other great ideas to make the BSC even better.

The BSC started taking shape one day when Kristy's mum was trying to find a babysitter for Kristy's younger brother, David Michael. (Kristy also has two older brothers, Charlie and Sam.) At the time, Mrs Thomas was going it alone as a single mum, as Kristy's dad had walked out on the family years earlier. Anyway, Kristy watched her mum make phone call after phone call without success, and that's when she came up with the idea for the BSC. She thought parents would love it if they could make one phone call and be guaranteed a responsible sitter. And she was right. Boy, was she right! Our club meets three times a week, on Mondays, Wednesdays and Fridays, from five-thirty till six. During those times, parents can phone to arrange sitting jobs. Using our club record book, we can work out who's free and schedule the jobs. It's as simple as that. The club's been a success right from the start, but Kristy couldn't leave well enough alone. She had to add more ideas, like the club notebook, in which we each write up every job we go on. This is my favourite thing about the BSC—*not*! Actually, it drives me crazy, because I'm not the world's best speller, and I'm sometimes embarrassed by my entries. Still, I have to admit that knowing the details of what's going on in our clients' lives makes us all better sitters.

Another patented Kristy Thomas idea? Kid-Kits. Those are boxes full of toys, stickers and games we bring along on jobs. I've just redecorated mine to look like a pirate ship. Kids *love* Kid-Kits.

Kristy knows what kids love, as kids are a big part of her life. Her mum remarried not that long ago, and when she did, Kristy's family doubled in size. Her stepfather, Watson Brewer, happens to be a millionaire—really! And Kristy moved to the other side of town to live in his mansion. He's got two kids, Karen and Andrew, from his first marriage. They live at Kristy's house every other month. Also, Kristy has a new *adopted* sister, Emily Michelle, who's Vietnamese. So that mansion is pretty full, especially when you add Kristy's grandmother Nannie, who came to live there and help out after Emily Michelle arrived, and all the pets (a puppy, a cat, two goldfish and two part-time pets, a rat and a hermit crab).

"How's Miss Vice-Chairman today?" asked Kristy, after she'd taken her usual seat in the director's chair near my desk.

I'm vice-chairman of the BSC. I was elected to that position because of one important thing: I'm the only member who has her own phone, with a private line. Besides answering the phone and arranging jobs during non-meeting times, my only other duty seems to be providing snacks for meetings. (That day I had dug out a box of jaw-breakers, a packet of fig rolls and some pretzels.)

"I'm fine," I said, answering Kristy's question. Then I held up a finger. "The door's just slammed again. I bet that's Stacey. I can hear her clogs." Stacey's just got this really cool pair of blue suede clogs. We'd featured them in the fashion shoot. I raised the camera to my eye and waited.

Sure enough, Stacey walked in a minute later. "Do the 'vogue'!" I cried. Without hesitating, Stacey struck a pose, tilting her face to the camera and letting her blonde, curly hair tumble down her back. *Snap!*

Right away, I was sure that anybody looking at the picture I'd just taken would *know* Stacey McGill. There she was, looking gorgeous and sophisticated, dressed in a totally up-to-the minute outfit. That's

16

Stacey. She grew up in Manhattan, and she still has that urban chic. She buys a lot of her clothes in the city, while she's visiting her dad. (Her parents are divorced. Stacey chose to live with her mum in Stoneybrook, but she sees her dad pretty regularly.)

Stacey is the BSC's treasurer, and she's the perfect person for the job. Get this—she actually *likes* maths class! She has a whale of a time collecting our subs, adding up all the money and then portioning it out for things like my phone bill and Kristy's transportation costs (her brother Charlie drives her to meetings). I wouldn't take that job if you paid me a million dollars, but Stacey does it just for the fun of it. I suppose it takes all kinds.

If you looked *very* carefully at the picture of Stacey, you might be able to see a certain glow. That's because she's got a boyfriend these days, called Robert. I'm happy for her, I really am. But I have to admit I'm also a bit jealous. First, because *I'd* like a boyfriend, too. I've even gone so far as to *advertise* for one, in this personal column I run for our school paper! But also because Stacey has been spending a *lot* of time with Robert. We had a big argument about that recently, but of course we made up. We always do. That's how best friends operate.

One thing you *wouldn't* be able to tell about Stacey, just by looking at the picture, is that she's got diabetes. Diabetes is a lifetime thing, but it doesn't *show*. I'd never have known if Stacey hadn't told us. Diabetes is a complicated disease to explain, and as I'm not exactly Doctor Science, I'll just say that Stacey's body doesn't handle sugar well, so she has to be very careful about what she eats. She also has to give herself injections (ouch!) of this stuff called insulin, just to keep things working properly. Diabetes is a very serious disease, but Stacey handles it well.

For example, that afternoon, after she had stopped posing and flopped down on my bed, Stacey helped herself to a pretzel, ignoring the jawbreakers and fig rolls. Then she smiled up at me. "Better focus on the door again," she said. "Somebody else is coming."

Sure enough, I heard footsteps on the stairs. Kristy, Stacey and I listened for a second. The footsteps weren't as "thumpy" as Kristy's had been. In fact, they sounded a bit tentative.

"Mary Anne!" we all said at the same time. I picked up the camera again and focused. When Mary Anne walked in and saw me looking at her through the camera, she immediately threw her hands over her face. *Snap!*

Another perfect shot. The picture would show Mary Anne's short dark hair (she and Kristy, her best friend, have similar colouring, but Mary Anne has a much cooler haircut) and her carefully chosen outfit (not *too* trendy, but much more thought-out than Kristy's). But it would also show something about Mary Anne's personality. If I had to choose one word to describe Mary Anne Spier, it would be this: shy. If I could pick a few more words, I'd add: sensitive, good listener, romantic and really sweet.

She's also an *excellent* club secretary. Mary Anne is in charge of the BSC record book, and she does a great job, keeping track of all our schedules and jobs.

Mary Anne grew up as the only child of a widower. Her mother died when Mary Anne was very young, and Mr Spier brought her up all by himself. Now, I've known Mary Anne (and Kristy, too, for that matter) all my life, and I have to say I've seen her go through some big changes. For one thing, her dad was *very* overprotective for a long time. He treated her like a little girl until she was at least twelve. But Mary Anne isn't a little girl any more, and I think her dad knows that now. She's got a steady boyfriend (a real sweetheart called Logan Bruno), and a mind of her own. Like Kristy, Mary Anne also has a new family. Her dad remarried, and his wife—Mary Anne's stepmother—happens to be the mother of another BSC member, Dawn Schafer, who is Mary Anne's *other* best friend. If I could snap a picture of Dawn, it would show a pretty, self-assured girl with long, long, blonde hair and a sunny smile. She'd probably be wearing something casual but cool.

How Dawn became Mary Anne's stepsister—and why I *can't* snap a picture of her—is rather a complicated story, so stay with me, okay? Here goes. Dawn's mum grew up in Stoneybrook, and went out with Mr Spier when they were both at high school. Then, she moved out to California, got married, and had two kids (Dawn and her younger brother Jeff). Unfortunately, the marriage didn't last, and after the divorce Dawn's mum moved back to Stoneybrook, with Jeff and Dawn in tow.

Dawn and Mary Anne became instant friends, discovered that their parents used to date, and brought them back together. Eventually, Richard (Mary Anne's dad) and Sharon (Dawn's mum) got married, and the two families settled into the old farmhouse where Dawn and her mum had been living. Sounds like a case of happy ever after, right?

Well, not exactly. I mean, they *are* happy, but there's more to the story. First, even before the wedding, Dawn's brother decided that he'd *never* adjust to living in Stoneybrook. He ended up going back to California to live with his dad. Then, not too long ago, Dawn realized that she was really, *really* missing Jeff and her dad, so she went out there, too. Not forever, though. Just for a long visit. We all miss her, but I know Mary Anne misses her the most of all.

When Dawn is in Stoneybrook, her BSC job is alternate officer. That means she can cover for any other officer who can't make it to a meeting. While Dawn's away, her position has been temporarily taken by Shannon Kilbourne, who is ordinarily one of our associate members. The other is Logan Bruno, Mary Anne's heartthrob. A photo of *him* would show a curly-haired, long-legged, very cute guy. It *wouldn't* show his adorable Kentucky accent, though. Associate members, by the way, don't always come to meetings. That's why I couldn't take a picture of Logan that day. He usually just helps out when we've got too many jobs to handle.

Anyway, Shannon walked in right behind Mary Anne that afternoon, and I hardly had time to raise my camera again. But fortunately, she stopped in the doorway for a second and glanced around the room. *Snap!*

I had her. Shannon has blonde hair, a turned-up nose, and a mischievious twinkle in her eyes. But she also has a serious side—she's one of the best students at her private school—and it would show in that snapshot. None of us knew Shannon very well until she started to come to meetings more regularly. She lives in Kristy's new neighbourhood and, as I mentioned, she doesn't go to SMS. But now that we know her, we all like her a lot. She's got two little sisters too, so she's great with kids, an important requirement for a BSC member.

Shannon had only just reached her seat on the floor near the foot of my bed, when I heard *more* footsteps and a gale of giggles coming from the stairs. I aimed the camera quickly, and shot our junior officers Jessi Ramsey and Mallory Pike as, still giggling, they squeezed through the door together. *Snap! Snap!*

Those two pictures would tell a lot. For one thing, both girls were in both pictures, and that's typical. Jessi and Mal stick together like glue, as they're best friends. Here's what else the photos would tell: that they're a little younger than the rest of the BSC members (we're thirteen, they're eleven), that Mal's got curly hair and glasses (you *wouldn't* see her brace in the picture as it's the clear kind, and you'd miss the fact that her hair is reddish-brown) and that

Jessi is African-American, with the prettiest coal-dark eyes. You'd see the pile of books Mal was carrying and guess that she loves reading. (So does Jessi. Horse stories are their favourites.) The sketch pad on top of the pile might give you a clue that Mal is a talented artist. And you'd know that Jessi has studied ballet for years, by the way she performed a quick but very graceful *plié* (that's French for, um, bend-the-knee) for the camera.

So, once again, I think I did pretty well at capturing those two. Here are some other things that wouldn't show up in the pictures: Jessi has a sweet younger sister called Becca and an adorable baby brother called Squirt (his real name is John Philip Ramsey, Jr). She also has an Aunt Cecelia, who lives with the family. Mal has *seven* siblings: Adam, Jordan, Byron, Vanessa, Nicky, Margo and Claire. Phew! Just saying their names makes me tired.

As soon as Jessi and Mal arrived that day, Kristy called the meeting to order. And as soon as Kristy called the meeting to order, the phone began to ring. And ring. And ring. As it's summer and all the kids are out of school, parents need us more than ever.

As each call came in, Mary Anne checked the record book to see who was free. Finally, at five minutes to six, the phone stopped ringing, and she gave a huge sigh. "Phew!"

she said, looking over the schedule. "We are *booked*!"

Kristy nodded, smiling, "Cool," she said.

"Except for one thing," said Mary Anne. "I hope we can make some time for a special project. I sat for the Barrett kids yesterday, and they were talking about that video we made for Dawn. Remember? Anyway, you know how crazy they were about her. They really miss her, and they want to make something else for her. Something that will make her homesick for Stoneybrook, so she'll come back sooner. Buddy is *dying* to have her back here."

I raised my camera and took another picture of Mary Anne right then, knowing that it would show that Buddy wasn't the only one who wanted Dawn back in Connecticut. Mary Anne had an "I miss Dawn" look all over her.

We tossed around some ideas for a project, but didn't come up with anything that seemed right. We agreed to give it some thought and talk about it again at our next meeting.

"I hope you'll have those pictures you took today to show us then, too," Kristy said to me.

"Absolutely," I said. I couldn't wait to get back into the darkroom and develop the roll I'd just shot. If I could manage it, I'd print up a whole series of pictures and have them displayed by the time everybody came over again. All I had to do was take one last picture, and I did that as soon as everybody had left. I faced the mirror, held the camera out to one side, and squeezed the shutter. Now I had a complete set (except for Dawn and Logan, of course). *A Portrait of the BSC*, I'd call it. And the subtitle would be, *My Best Friends*.

3rd CHAPTER

Saturday

This is the best idea yet! Dawn is going to love, love, love it. I wish we could start on it today! This will be one of the most creative projects the BSC has ever taken on. It should be, since it took ten kids and three baby-sitters to think it up...

Mary Anne's entry in the club notebook goes on and on, but I'll spare you the rest of her gushing. Actually, I was as excited as she was about the idea we hatched that Saturday afternoon. In fact, I was one of the three sitters who were in on thinking it up—but maybe I should start at the beginning.

Mary Anne had a sitting job with Buddy, Suzi and Marnie Barrett that day. (Buddy's eight, Suzi's five and Marnie's two, and together they can be *quite* a handful. They used to be known as the Impossible Three.) Like a good BSC member, Mary Anne always arrives at her job a little early, so she turned up at the Barretts' house at the same time as Franklin DeWitt. Who's Franklin DeWitt? He's not one of the Founding Fathers, although to me his name always sounds like one I should have remembered for a history test. He *is* a father, though. A father who has custody of his four kids. And he was going to the Barretts' because he's Mrs Barretts' boyfriend, and he was picking her up for a date. Mrs Barrett is a single (divorced) mum.

Mr DeWitt and Mrs Barrett seem to be pretty serious about each other these days. Sometimes my friends and I speculate about what it would be like if they got married. The Brady Bunch would have nothing on the Barrett-DeWitt bunch!

Buddy answered the door when Mr DeWitt knocked, but instead of saying hello to his mum's boyfriend, Buddy ignored him completely. He ran right past Franklin to Mary Anne. "Mary Anne!" he said. "Have you come up with an idea yet? It has to be a really, really good one!"

Mary Anne, shocked at Buddy's bad manners, was just about to tell Buddy to say hello to Mr DeWitt, but then Mrs Barrett did it for her. "Buddy Barrett," she began, standing in the doorway with her hands on her hips. Mary Anne told me later that Mrs Barrett looked gorgeous, as always, this time in a simple white dress with her beautiful chestnut hair flowing loose.

Mrs Barrett could be a model, honestly.

However, as she stood there glaring at Buddy, she looked more angry than anything else. "Can't you say hello to Franklin?" she said. "Where are your manners, young man?"

Buddy hung his head. "Hi, Mr DeWitt," he said, not meeting Franklin's eyes. "Sorry. It's just that I had something really important to ask Mary Anne about, and—"

"That's okay, Buddy," said Mr DeWitt, smiling. Then he turned to Mrs Barrett. "We'd better leave now if we want to get good seats."

"We're going to an outdoor concert in Stamford," Mrs Barrett told Mary Anne, "so you won't be able to reach us. But I've left an emergency phone number on the kitchen table."

"Thanks," said Mary Anne. We always appreciate it when Mrs Barrett remembers to do things like that. She used to be pretty scatterbrained, but recently she's been trying harder. Maybe it's partly Mr DeWitt's influence.

Suzy and Marnie came out on to the porch to say goodbye to the grown-ups, and they and their brother waved as Franklin's car pulled out of the drive. Mary Anne confessed to me later that Mrs Barrett's white dress made her think of weddings, and she actually had a tear in her eye as she watched the two of them drive off.

Mary Anne never misses an opportunity to get sentimental.

"So, how are the DeWitt kids?" she asked Buddy, as soon as she'd composed herself.

"Fine, I think," said Buddy. "Now what about that idea? You know, for Dawn?"

Mary Anne smiled. Obviously, Buddy only had one thing on his mind. "Well, I told everybody in the BSC about how you wanted to do something, and they agreed that we should come up with a project."

29

"So what's it going to be?" asked Buddy.

"Yeah, what shall we do?" said Suzi.

"Do!" echoed Marnie.

"That's the only problem," Mary Anne admitted. "We haven't thought of anything yet."

Buddy's face fell. "Oh," he said.

"But I'll tell you what," said Mary Anne. "Claudia's over at the Pikes', helping Mal sit for her brothers and sisters. Why don't we go over there? I bet if all of us think hard, we can come up with a terrific idea."

"Yea!" said Buddy. "Let's go *right now*!"

"Mum said you have to feed all the pets before you go anywhere," Suzi reminded him.

"Merturple!" said Marnie.

"Mer—*what*?" asked Mary Anne.

"She means Mr Turtle," explained Buddy. "He's her favourite. I like Frisky best, though."

"Frisky's the gerbil," Suzi said. "But he's not really very frisky. Mostly he sleeps."

Mary Anne followed the kids to their playroom, where all the animals are kept. Buddy and Suzi fed them, introducing the new ones to Mary Anne. The Barretts used to have a dog, a funny-looking basset hound called Pow. But then Marnie became allergic to dogs, and they had to give Pow away. (Happily, he didn't go far. In fact, the Barretts would be seeing their beloved mutt that day, as it was the Pikes who took him.) Anyway, now the kids have an ever-expanding menagerie of *non*-allergenic pets, and that day Mary Anne met them all, including the fifteen guppies named after famous baseball players.

At last all the pets were fed. Mary Anne left a note for Mrs Barrett, and then she and the kids went over to the Pikes' house, which is just down the road from the Barretts'. When they arrived, Mal and I were sitting on the front porch, watching the Pike kids do their thing.

"Doing their thing" means something different for each of the Pike kids. Here's how the scene looked that afternoon: for starters, Jordan and Adam, two of the ten-year-old identical triplets, were teasing Nicky, who's eight, about his new haircut.

"You look like one of those cactuses out West," said Adam.

"I do not!" said Nicky.

"Cactus-head!" said Jordan.

Nicky stuck out his tongue. "I know I am, but what are you?" he sang.

Jordan and Adam shouted with laughter. "That's backward, cactus-head," said Adam. "You're supposed to say "I know *you* are but what am *I*?""

"I know that," said Nicky, with dignity.

31

He walked away from them—they were still laughing—and joined his younger sisters, Margo (seven) and Claire (five), who were busy dressing up Pow as a baby.

"Can you help us tuck him into the pram?" Margo asked. "Every time we try to squish one part of him in, another part sticks out." Nicky was glad to stay and help, if only to avoid more teasing from his brothers.

Meanwhile, Byron, the third triplet, was trying to retrieve a Frisbee from the porch roof, with Mal watching anxiously as he climbed along the gutter. Vanessa, who's nine, was sitting on the porch rocking chair, oblivious to the chaos. She's wanted to be a poet for as long as any of us can remember, and she's happiest when she's scribbling in one of her notebooks.

When Mary Anne arrived with the Barrett kids, the first thing Buddy did was say hi to Pow. "He'll stay in the pram if you give him a doggie chew," he advised the girls and Nicky. Then he joined us on the porch, and he and Mary Anne told us why they had come.

Almost at once, all the Pike kids dropped what they were doing and came over to join the discussion. Vanessa turned to a new page in her notebook, in order to take down ideas. Byron came down from the roof, without the Frisbee but with two softballs he'd found. Claire and Margo set Pow free, and Nicky, Jordan and Adam made up and sat down to brainstorm.

That's what Mary Anne called it: brainstorming. "We did brainstorming in my social studies class last year," she said. "It's the best way to come up with ideas. Everybody just shouts out anything they can think of, no matter how silly it is. You'd be surprised at the creative stuff we'll come up with."

Naturally, after that, there were a few minutes of total silence. Nobody wanted to shout out the first silly idea. At last I decided to jump right in. "We could send an aeroplane over Dawn's favourite beach, towing one of those big, long banners. It could say 'DAWN SCHAFER, PLEASE COME HOME TO STONEYBROOK'!"

"Uh-huh," said Vanessa, writing it down. Nobody else said a word.

"Well, you said we could say silly ideas," I said, blushing.

Just then, Buddy piped in. "If we put all our money together, maybe we could buy her a plane ticket home."

"Yeah!" said Nicky. "I've got . . ." he dug in his pocket, "seventeen cents."

"And I've got three dollars in my piggy bank upstairs!" said Adam.

"I think it's going to cost a lot more than that," said Mal gently.

"Okay," said Jordan, "speaking of planes, how about this? We'll hire a plane to fly over Stoneybrook and take one of those pictures from above. Then we'll frame it and send it to her."

"That's pretty expensive, too," said Mary Anne. "Anyway, it should be something we can *make* for her."

The kids continued brainstorming, shouting out ideas for everything from a singing telegram to a giant mural to a parcel of homemade biscuits.

"I've got it!" I shouted, after a few more minutes. I'd been thinking hard, ever since Jordan had mentioned pictures. As I've got photography on the brain at the moment, my ears had pricked up when I heard that word. "You know that book, *A Day in the Life of America*?"

"You mean the one where they gave a lot of photographers one day to take pictures all over the country?" Mal said. "We've got that book. It's pretty cool."

"Well, how about *A Day in the Life of Stoneybrook*?" I asked. "We can fix up a lot of you kids with cameras—I'm sure we can borrow a few—and you can take pictures all over town. Then we'll make up an album for Dawn."

"Yeah," said Buddy, starting to grin. "Yeah! I like it."

Mal went to find the book. When she

brought it back, the kids handed it around and looked at it. They loved it, so the matter was decided. We agreed to round up more photographers—all clients and members of the BSC—and we set our "day" for the following Sunday.

That night, Mary Anne couldn't resist phoning Dawn. "The kids are planning a big surprise for you," she told her stepsister. "And you're going to *love* it." Then she rang me, and we talked about the project some more. I think Mary Anne and I were even more excited than any one of the kids who'd been over at the Pikes' that day, but *none* of us could wait for next Sunday.

4th CHAPTER

Before I went home that Saturday, I borrowed the Pikes' copy of *A Day in the Life of America*. Later, when I sat down and looked it over more closely, I began to realize that our project was going to take a *lot* of planning. For the real *Day in the Life* book, the editors had asked two hundred of the world's top photographers to take pictures all over America during one twenty-four-hour period. From what I read, it took a huge amount of coordination to pull that together.

We weren't using two hundred photographers for *A Day in the Life of Stoneybrook*, but there was still a lot to work out. My friends and I spent every spare minute that week plotting and planning for our big day on Sunday. First, we rang around to find out which of our regular charges wanted to be part of the project. Then we

36

rounded up all the cameras we could find, so that each kid would be able to take pictures. I borrowed Janine's instamatic, and Mary Anne dug out her dad's old Brownie camera. The Pikes had a Polaroid, and Stacey and her mum volunteered their instant camera. Shannon was going to use her automatic, and Watson lent Kristy his fancy Nikon, after she promised to take good care of it. We also took some money out of the BSC treasury to buy films and a couple of disposable cameras.

And finally, we sat down with the club record book and worked out a schedule for the shoot. Not everybody in the BSC would be available that day. Logan was going away for the weekend with his family, and Stacey was going to New York to visit her dad. (She'd be coming back late on Sunday afternoon, though, so we planned to meet her at the railway station and take pictures of her arrival.) Kristy had a softball game with her team, the Krushers, first thing in the morning. Since many of the kids who wanted to be part of the project are also Krushers, we decided to meet on the ballfield on Sunday morning. We would take some pictures of the game, and then split up into smaller groups to cover the rest of Stoneybrook.

I woke up early on Sunday morning and,

with my fingers crossed, jumped straight out of bed to pull up my blinds. As soon as I saw the blue sky outside, I grinned. It was a perfect day, just what we'd been hoping for. I dressed quickly, in jeans and my "Hard Rock Cafe" T-shirt (no high fashion today; I was planning to work hard) and started to load my camera bag. I'd be shooting in black and white, as I wanted to be able to develop my pictures myself, and I had stocked up on film. I stuck two rolls into the outside pocket of my bag and loaded a third into the Minolta. Our *Day in the Life of Stoneybrook* was about to begin, and I was ready.

I was itching to start taking pictures, so I left my room with the camera around my neck. Just as I was heading for the stairs, I heard the bathroom door open. I whirled around, raised my camera, and started snapping away.

"Claudia!" cried Janine. "What do you think you're *doing*?" At least, that's what it sounded like. Her words were rather garbled.

I lowered the camera and took a better look at her. She was wearing this ratty old pink dressing gown that she refuses to give up, and there was a yellow towel wrapped turban-style around her head. Her voice had sounded funny because she was in the middle of brushing her teeth and her mouth was full of foamy white toothpaste.

"Oops!" I said, trying to hide a grin. "Hey, it's all just part of our project, Janine!" I said. "Don't you want to be included? I can see the caption saying something like 'Janine Kishi prepares for her day, looking forward to—' hey, what *are* you doing today?" I asked.

"Going on a picnic with Jerry," she said. "And if you assume I'm going to reveal our destination, you're most definitely mistaken." She shook her toothbrush at me and stomped back into the bathroom.

Jerry is Janine's boyfriend. For a second I thought about trying to follow them and take candid shots without their seeing me, but then I remembered the very full schedule we'd made up for the day. There was no way I could fit anything else in. I shrugged and went downstairs, where I quickly snapped pictures of my dad making waffles and my mum reading the Sunday paper. As soon as I'd finished my breakfast, I grabbed my camera bag and made my way over to the ballfield.

The Krushers were playing Bart's Bashers that day. Bart Taylor, the guy who manages the Bashers, is Kristy's boyfriend—although she'd kill me if she heard me say that. She insists she's "not into that boyfriend-girlfriend stuff". The game was nearly over when I arrived, and the scene at the field was totally chaotic.

Buddy Barrett was on first base, and Suzi was up at bat. Jamie Newton, who's four, was waiting for his turn to hit. He was holding a blue plastic camera (the kind made for kids) and trying to focus on Kristy and Bart, who were talking over on the sidelines. Charlotte Johanssen, who's nine, was leading cheers, along with Haley Braddock (also nine) and Vanessa Pike. Becca, Jessi's sister, had talked them into making a mini-pyramid for a picture she wanted to take, but the pyramid kept collapsing because the girls were giggling too much.

I found Jessi, Mal, Shannon and Mary Anne sitting together by the field. "Have you lot started taking pictures yet?" I asked.

"Absolutely," said Jessi, grinning. "I caught Aunt Cecelia in her fuzzy slippers, Shannon took some pictures of her sister playing dressing up, and Mary Anne has already taken a roll and a half of Tigger playing with a toy mouse." Tigger is Mary Anne's kitten.

"You should have seen Nicky this morning," Mal said, laughing. "He was trying to take a picture of Pow. First he tied this huge red bow around Pow's neck. Then he got ready to snap a picture. He'd tell Pow to sit, and then he'd walk away a few steps in order to focus. But as soon as Nicky was ready to take the picture, Pow would get up, walk towards him, and stick his big old snuffly nose right up against the camera. It was hilarious!"

Suddenly, we heard cheering on the field, and we all turned to see what had happened. An ecstatic Matt Braddock was circling the bases, while his sister Haley signed frantically to him. "What's she telling him?" I asked Jessi. Matt is profoundly deaf, and he and Haley (and most of his friends) communicate with American Sign Language. Jessi has learned ASL better than anyone else in the BSC.

"She's saying 'It's a home run! We win!'" said Jessi. "But from the look on Matt's face, I've a feeling he already knows that."

"Now he'll really have something to tell everybody about at that picnic today," I said. Matt and Haley's parents were hosting a picnic for hearing-impaired children and their families that afternoon. The kids were mostly from Matt's school, which is in Stamford. Shannon and Kristy were going along, and they'd take pictures of the event for our project.

As soon as the Krushers and Bashers had finished their post-game rituals (lining up to give high fives to the other team, and then chanting "two-four-six-eight! Who do we appreciate?"), Kristy, Shannon, Mary Anne, Mal, Jessi and I held a quick meeting.

"Have you all got your cameras?" Kristy asked, after we'd congratulated her on the game.

We nodded and held them up.

"Film?" asked Kristy. When we nodded, she grinned. "Then let's go!" she said. She and Shannon headed off with Matt and Haley, while Jessi and Mal rounded up Nicky, Vanessa and Jamie Newton. The Jessi-and-Mal team was planning to go over to the barber's shop in town, where the triplets had haircut appointments.

"I can't wait to call them cactus-heads," I heard Nicky saying as they set off.

Mary Anne and I called Buddy, Suzi, Charlotte and Becca together and made sure they all knew how to use the cameras they were holding. Then we set off for the town centre. At first, the kids just kept snapping pictures of each other as we walked. Suzi told Buddy to say "cheese", and then she snapped his picture while Becca held up two fingers behind his head. "Rabbit ears!" Charlotte giggled. Then Charlotte flapped both her hands behind *Becca's* head while Buddy snapped the picture. "Moose ears!" Suzi shrieked. Soon they were all giggling so hard they could hardly hold up their cameras.

"Hey, you lot," said Mary Anne, when we got to town. "Why don't you look around? There's lots of interesting stuff to take pictures of."

Mary Anne was right. As soon as we started to look at what was going on around us, we saw amazing things. First, Suzi spotted a wedding party having their pictures taken in a little park. Then, Buddy caught sight of a really cool red sports car parked in front of the hardware shop. Charlotte took a picture of the window of Polly's Fine Candy, where there was a display of fancy boxed chocolates. And Becca took some arty shots of the Rosebud Cafe's neon sign. Mary Anne was photographing *everything*, including the mannequins in the window of the Merry-Go-Round. (She took so many pictures that she ran out of film and had to borrow some of mine.) And me? I was taking picture after picture of the façades of central Stoneybrook.

A façade, in case you don't know, is the front of a building. (It's pronounced fah-*sahd*, by the way. Don't ask me why.) Some are plain, but some are really, really fancy. The fancy ones have stone carvings of vines or flowers or even people. There might be building names etched over the doorway, or numbers carved into the sides. Looking through my camera's viewfinder, I was amazed. I had never noticed all those details before, even though I've been in central Stoneybrook about three million times. As Mr Giest says, sometimes you see things completely differently when you look at them through a camera.

I was especially fascinated with the façade of the old Stoneybrook bank building. It had vines and flowers *and* words, as well as marble pillars and beautiful old revolving doors trimmed with brass. As the sun shone on the building, it cast really cool shadows over the carvings. I shot photo after photo of the bank, going through one whole roll of film and starting on a second. At one point, I noticed Mary Anne taking pictures of *me* taking pictures. She seemed to think that what I was doing looked funny. I just ignored her.

By then, I wasn't even thinking of Dawn or our project any more. Instead, I had become obsessed with "capturing the essence" of that building, just as if it were a person I was taking a portrait of. I was even hatching a whole new project that I couldn't wait to present to Mr Geist: a portfolio of building portraits. I knew he'd love it.

I had forgotten about Mary Anne and the kids until suddenly I felt a tug at my sleeve. "Claudia!" said Buddy. "What are you doing? Come *on*."

"Yeah, come on," said Charlotte. "We've already used up all our film. And we took much more interesting pictures than *you're* taking." She glanced at the bank. "I mean, that's just a boring old building."

I tried to explain why the building fascinated me, but Mary Anne and the kids kept teasing me. At last Mary Anne pointed out that we needed to break for lunch *soon* if we were going to be at the railway station in time to meet Stacey's train. I took one last picture of the bank, and we set off for lunch at the Rosebud Cafe.

Later that afternoon, we all met up in my room to talk about how the day had worked out. Shannon and Kristy reported that they'd each taken some great shots at the picnic, and Jessi and Mal were thrilled about their pictures of the triplets' haircuts. Mary Anne told everybody about my obsession with the bank, and they teased me, but I didn't let it bother me. I just said to them, "Wait and see. Those pictures are going to turn out *great*!"

Little did we know (I love that phrase!) that those pictures would turn out to be very, *very* important.

5th CHAPTER

"Baby, baby, angel of mine, my heart is in your hands—" Stacey and I waltzed around my room together, crooning along with the radio. When the song ended, we fell on to my bed, giggling.

"I *adore* that song," I said.

"Me, too," said Stacey. "It reminds me of Robert."

"Oh, Robert, Robert, Robert," I said, grabbing a pillow and bopping her with it. We giggled some more.

"Order!" said Kristy, suddenly.

"Is it five-thirty *already*?" I asked. I glanced at the clock on my bedside table. Sure enough, it was time for our BSC meeting. It was a Wednesday, three days after we'd done all that picture-taking, and my friends were gathered in my room for our meeting. I still hadn't had a chance to develop the photos I'd taken on Sunday, mostly because I'd been working on my portrait series. The pictures of my friends were almost ready, and I could hardly wait.

Kristy reached over and snapped the radio off.

"No!" I cried, snapping it back on. "You can't do that!"

"Why not?" she asked. "It's time for our meeting."

"I know," I said. "But WSTO is playing a whole hour of Billy Blue right now. There's no way I'm missing *that*."

"Who's Billy Blue?" asked Kristy.

"WHO'S BILLY BLUE?" Stacey and I shouted together.

"Kristy, I don't believe you," Stacey said. "Sometimes I think you live under a *rock* or something. Billy Blue is *only* the best singer since—since—"

"We're wasting time here," said Kristy impatiently. "How about this? We can leave the radio on, but you'll have to turn it down."

"Cool," I said. I reached over and inched the volume control down, just the tiniest bit.

"Lower," said Kristy, giving me a Look.

"Okay, okay," I said, turning it way down. I could still hear Billy Blue, but only just. Still, it was better than nothing. Right then he was singing another song I love, called "Your Sweet Kiss". Stacey and I grinned at each other as we mouthed the words silently. Kristy ignored us.

"Any new business?" she asked.

Nobody said anything. Stacey and I started to sing very softly along with Billy. Kristy reached over as if to turn the radio off again, and we broke off in mid-song. "Sorry! Sorry!" I said. "We'll stop, I promise."

Kristy just gave me another Look and turned to ask Stacey about the state of the treasury. "My Kid-Kit is almost due for some new stickers and markers," she said. "Have we got enough money?"

"Of course," said Stacey, instantly serious. She always knows exactly—and I mean to the last *penny*—how much is in the Treasury. "I need some stickers, too."

"We should plan a shopping trip," said Mary Anne. "I've run out of those little colouring books, and Suzi Barrett has a *fit* if I turn up without one."

"Have you got a job with them soon?" asked Shannon.

"With the Barretts *and* the DeWitts," said Mary Anne. "Kristy and I are sitting for both families together next week."

"Whoa!" said Jessi. "That should be a challenge."

Just then, Billy Blue stopped singing, and this time Kristy wasn't responsible. "We interrupt this programme for a special announcement," I heard an announcer say. I held up my hand. "Hey, listen, you lot!" I said.

"This is *exactly* why I don't want the radio playing during—" Kristy began, but Stacey shushed her. She had just heard the same thing I had heard—a mention of the Stoneybrook Bank.

"Hold on, Kristy," she said. "This could be important."

I turned up the volume, and we all listened.

"A recent surprise audit has uncovered a major deficit in the bank's holdings," the reporter said, sounding very serious. I wasn't exactly sure what she meant by that, but as she kept talking, it became pretty clear. There was a *ton* of money missing from the bank, and no way to explain why.

"Hundreds of thousands of dollars," Mallory whispered, echoing the reporter's words. "I can't even imagine what that much money *looks* like."

The reporter went on to say that the police had already ruled out the possibility of "transaction error" (Stacey said that meant, like, if a clerk had put ten too many zeros after a number or something), and that the bank's video cameras showed no signs of a robbery or forcible entry. Then she said that the bank was asking for anybody with information or tips to phone a special number. Then the announcement ended, and Billy Blue came back on, in the middle of singing "I'm Lost Without You".

This time, *I* was the one to reach over and turn the radio off. Kristy looked at me in amazement. "That was big news," I said. "I mean, that could be *our* money that's missing."

"Have you got an account at that bank?" asked Shannon.

"Well, no," I admitted. "But I *might* have opened one, if I ever decided to save my money. Anyway, I was just thinking— wouldn't it be great if there was a clue to the crime in one of those pictures I took on Sunday? I mean, I must have shot a zillion pictures of that bank."

"Oh, Claud, you've been watching too many late-night films," said Stacey.

"There *is* a film about something like that happening," Mary Anne said thoughtfully. "I can't think of the title, but it's about this photographer who takes a picture of a murder—by mistake, I mean. He only finds out about it later, when he develops the pictures."

"You see?" I said. "It could happen."

"Of course it could," said Kristy. "But it doesn't seem too likely. I mean, we don't even know when the crime took place. It'd

50

be a major coincidence if it happened last Sunday."

"Kristy's right," said Stacey. "I mean, this isn't *Nancy Drew and the Mystery of the Bank*." She poked me in the side and giggled. The rest of my friends joined in the teasing, but I tried not to pay any attention.

"I don't care what you all say. I'm going to develop that film—tonight," I said.

And that's exactly what I did, straight after dinner that evening. Janine was out with Jerry, and she wasn't due home until pretty late that evening, so even though I hadn't got around to making that *Darkroom in Use* sign for the bathroom, I knew it would be safe to develop film in there. I arranged everything, stuffed the towel under the door, and turned out all the lights. I was only developing one roll of film. The other roll, which only had a few bank pictures, was still in my camera. It didn't take long to load the film in the tank, and once that was done I turned the lights back on and got to work with the chemicals.

When the film was finished, I hung it up to dry. I could tell that the pictures were all clear and that the developing had gone well, but I wouldn't be able to have a good look at them till the film was dry and I could make a contact print. I left the darkroom and got to work on my maths homework. Then I had a snack (some Fritos, with a Three Musketeers bar for dessert) and read a few chapters of *The Clue of the Tapping Heels*, one of my all-time favourite Nancy Drew books. I think I must have read that one about four times, but I still love it.

At last, at about ten-thirty, I decided the film must be dry. I knew my parents wouldn't be too keen on my working in the darkroom that late, but I couldn't resist going in to make a quick contact print.

A contact print is a great way to look at negatives. Here's how you make it: you just lay the negatives down on a piece of photographic paper, shine some light on them, and then develop the paper. In order to see what you're doing during this kind of work you use a "safelight"—a red light that doesn't ruin pictures. I just replace the bulb in the bathroom light with a special red one. When you've finished, what you have is a print of the negatives that you can look at with an eyeglass, so you can tell which shots might be worth enlarging.

My heart was beating fast as I made the contact print and developed it. Then I hung it up to dry—but I was too impatient to wait. Even though it was still damp, I brought it out to my desk and started to peer at each picture through the eyeglass. I examined them one by one, and by the time I finished, my heart wasn't beating so fast any more.

The pictures didn't show a thing.

Oh, there were some great shots of the bank's façade, with its columns and carvings. And there were a few people in the pictures, too: a mother pushing a baby's pram appeared in a lot of them, and so did a man in a suit. But that was it. What a let-down!

The funny thing was this: during our meeting, my friends had been teasing me about the slim possibility of clues turning up in my pictures. But guess who turned up at my house as soon as I got home from summer school the next day? Kristy, Mary Anne and Stacey. They couldn't *wait* to see what I'd found on the roll of film. "Not much," I told them, showing them the contact print. One by one, they peered at the pictures through the eyeglass.

"You're right," Kristy said, after her turn. "Not much at all."

"I wonder how old the baby is," said Mary Anne, after she'd looked.

"That guy must be a banker," joked Stacey when she'd finished. "He's got one of those banker's pocket watches. You know, the kind that fastens to your belt with a chain."

"If he's a banker, why isn't he *in* the bank?" asked Kristy.

"I was only *kidding*," said Stacey.

Kristy took one last look at the pictures, and shook her head. "Drat! I was really hoping we'd get some clues," she said, smacking her fist into her palm.

"Oh, well," I said. I tried not to show how funny I thought it was that my friends had got all excited about the pictures, after teasing me for my interest. Instead, I decided to distract them. "Weren't we going to buy some new stuff for our Kid-Kits?" I asked. "Why don't we go into town now?" And that was that. We left about three minutes later, without a backward glance at that disappointing contact print lying on my desk.

6th CHAPTER

Friday

The mystery is growing. If this were a Nancy Drew book, what would the title be? The Bank Robbery Mystery? Mystery at the Bank?

How about The mistery of the Misplaced money?

Nice one, Claud. Anyway, this isn't a Nancy Drew book. If it were, the mystery would probably be solved by now. And we're nowhere near a solution.

Becka and sharlate sure do make cute detectives, though.

55

It was an absolutely *gorgeous* Friday afternoon. Blue sky, white puffy clouds, the whole bit. Hot, but not muggy. Just a perfect summer day.

Stacey was sitting for Jamie Newton and his baby sister Lucy while Mrs Newton visited an aunt who'd just got home from hospital.

"I've got something for you," Jamie said to Stacey. She was sitting on the front porch, keeping an eye on Lucy, who was bouncing in her baby seat. Jamie was standing on the bottom step, his hands behind his back.

"Have you?" asked Stacey, smiling. Jamie is one of our favourite charges. He's four, and he's as cute as a puppy. In fact, at that moment Stacey couldn't help but think of puppies when she looked at Jamie. He had this sweet, hopeful look in his eyes, just like a puppy who's angling for a treat. "What is it?" Stacey asked.

Jamie pulled a bunch of flowers from behind his back. "These!" he said. "I picked them myself!"

Stacey stared at the flowers, horrified. This was not a handful of dandelions or clover blossoms. This was a big bunch of flowers—with *roots* still attached!

"Jamie!" said Stacey. "Where did you *get* those?"

"From the flowerbed over there," Jamie

56

said, pointing towards the huge, colourful flowerbed Mrs Newton is so proud of.

"Oh, Jamie," said Stacey. "I *love* the flowers, I really do. But flowers need to stay in the ground."

Jamie looked crestfallen.

"Come on," said Stacey, giving him a hug. "I'll help you tuck them back in." She lifted Lucy out of the baby seat, carried her over near the flower beds, and put her down to crawl in the grass. Then she got to work replanting the flowers Jamie had pulled up. She stuck each one back into the ground, hoping that they would live. Then she watered them carefully and sat back to look. If Mrs Newton didn't check *too* closely, she might not notice the few wilted blooms amid her thriving plants.

"I'm sorry, Stacey," said Jamie. "I just wanted to give you a present." He frowned and rubbed at the chicken pox scar on his cheek. Jamie and Lucy both had chicken pox not that long ago."

"That's okay, Jamie," said Stacey. She glanced over at Lucy, who was busy pulling up grass. Lucy peered back with an innocent, "who, me?" look in her eyes. Stacey sighed. The Newton children seemed to be determined to destroy their garden that day. "How about if we take Miss Lucy Jane for a walk in her buggy?" Stacey asked Jamie. "We'll go and visit Claudia. She's babysitting for Charlotte Johanssen, around the corner."

"Yea!" said Jamie. "Claudee!" Jamie's always called me that.

Lucy smiled broadly, showing all four of her teeth. She knows what "walk" means, and she *loves* her buggy.

Stacey grabbed her rucksack, stuck an extra bottle and a nappy in it, and left a note for Mrs Newton. Then they were off. At first they went slowly, as Jamie insisted on pushing the buggy. "Lucy only likes it when *I* push," he said. After half a block, though, he was distracted by a beetle crawling on the pavement, and Stacey took over.

When the three of them arrived at the Johanssens', they found Charlotte and me out on the drive, along with Becca, who had come over to visit. We were taking turns bouncing a little red rubber ball and playing this game I'd taught them.

"A my name is Alice and my husband's name is Al," said Charlotte, bouncing the ball. "We come from Alabama, and we sell—uh—*apples*!"

Then Becca took over. "B my name is Bertha and my husband's name is Bart. We come from—from *Bermuda* and we sell baseball bats."

"My turn!" I said. I was having a great time. "C my name is Claudia," I said, grinning while I bounced the ball. "And my husband's name is Carl. We come from California and we sell cardigans!"

"Good job, Claud," said Stacey, applauding. She had sneaked up on us, and now she and Jamie stood clapping while Lucy grinned from her buggy. "But couldn't you have thought of something more creative to sell? Like canaries, maybe? Or cannonballs?"

"Cats!" shouted Jamie.

"Chipmunks!" yelled Becca, giggling.

"Clarinets!" said Charlotte. "Clouds! Coco Puffs!" She and Becca shrieked with laughter.

I laughed and bent to give Jamie, who was also doubled over with giggles, a hug. "Good to see you lot," I said. "What are you up to?"

"We're going for a walk!" said Jamie.

"Great idea!" I said.

"We want to walk, too," said Becca. "Let's *go* somewhere."

Stacey and I exchanged looks and shrugs. Both of us were sitting for the whole day, so it didn't matter much what we did. "I've been carrying around some small change," she said, "and I'm tired of my rucksack being so heavy. We could drop it off at the bank, and then maybe walk around town a little."

"Let's go! We can window-shop," said Becca.

"Shop for windows?" asked Jamie. "I don't want to buy any windows."

Giggling again, Becca explained what she'd meant.

"We could get some ice-cream, too," said Charlotte, licking her lips.

Stacey checked to make sure Lucy's nappy was dry and that she was comfortable in her buggy. I went inside and left a note for Dr Johanssen, Charlotte's mother. (We always leave notes, even if we don't expect the parents back for hours.)

We set off for town, with each of the three kids taking turns pushing Lucy's buggy. Lucy dozed off immediately, and Jamie kept himself busy counting everything—cracks in the pavements, cars in driveways—*everything*. As we walked, Stacey and the girls and I played the "A my name is Alice" game some more. We were getting sillier and sillier.

"G my name is Gertrude," I said, "and my husband's name is Gus. We come from Germany, and we sell giraffes."

"H my name is—is—is *Heather*," said Becca, "and my husband's name is Harry. We come from Honolulu, and we sell hangers."

By the time we reached central Stoneybrook, we'd been all the way through the alphabet and we were back at B again. Charlotte and Becca really cracked up when

Charlotte said her name was Bettina and that she and her husband Bob, who were from Baltimore, sold *bogies*.

"Okay, okay," said Stacey, trying to calm them down. "That's enough now. It's time to go into the bank, so let's quieten down a little, okay?"

Charlotte and Becca had one more explosion of giggles, but then they became serious. "Is this the bank all the money is missing from?" Charlotte asked, looking up at the fancy façade. I nodded. Charlotte is a clever little girl, and she doesn't miss much. I realized she must have overheard Stacey and me when we mentioned the bank mystery during the walk into town. Charlotte turned to Becca. "Let's be detectives," she said. "Quick, put on your disguise." She turned the baseball cap she was wearing back to front and grinned at Becca. Becca pulled a pair of sunglasses out of her pocket and put them on.

The three kids went through the revolving door—pushing it around and around until a guard gave them a sharp look—while Stacey and I manoeuvred Lucy's buggy through the ordinary doors. Then I waited with the kids while Stacey stood in a queue to pay in her cash. I looked around, wondering how it could be possible for such a well-guarded bank to be robbed.

"Look at all the policemen!" Jamie said, his eyes round as he examined the guards.

"They must have extra because of that money disappearing," said Charlotte.

Of course! Charlotte was right. There probably *were* more guards than usual.

"Look at that big cage over there," said Charlotte. "What's that for?"

I turned to see what she was looking at, and saw the vault for the safe-deposit boxes. The iron bars on the gate in front of it *did* look like a cage. I explained to Charlotte how safe-deposit boxes work, something I'd learned from going to the bank with my father. "People can rent those boxes to keep valuable things safe," I said. "You get your own key, and what you put in your box is your own private business. It's like a miniature safe." Charlotte thought that sounded pretty cool, and said she might get a safe-deposit box one day to keep her favourite Barbie in.

Just then, Becca-the-detective poked Charlotte. "Don't look now," she said, "but there's a *very* suspicious character over by the table there."

"Where?" asked Charlotte, looking around immediately.

"I *said*, don't look!" said Becca. "Never mind. He's gone already. But keep an eye out. I bet he'll be back. He had this big black moustache, and I'm sure it was fake."

While the girls kept busy playing detective and I kept busy watching Jamie and Lucy, Stacey waited in a long queue. I saw her tapping her foot impatiently as she waited. The next time I looked, she was at the top of the queue. And the *next* time I looked, she was hurrying towards us, her face bright red.

"Come on," she said, pulling me along. "Let's get out of here. I'm so embarrassed."

"What *happened*?" I asked her, once we were back out on the street with our charges in tow.

"You won't believe it," she said. "Remember that man in your pictures? The one in the suit, who I said was a banker?"

I nodded.

"I was only kidding, but it turns out that maybe I was *right*! He was standing behind the counter, talking to one of the bank clerks. I was so surprised to see him that I dropped some of my cash on my foot. My toe is *killing* me!" She paused. "Anyway, when I'd collected up the money and given it to the desk, the man had gone. And the clerk must have thought I was mad."

Just then, Lucy stretched in her buggy and began to whimper. Charlotte and Becca, bored with playing detectives, started to talk about buying ice-cream, and Jamie joined in. So Stacey and I took them to the Rosebud Cafe and bought them each a cone. Then, just as we were about to go home, Stacey remembered that the kids' pictures from Sunday might be ready, so we stopped at the camera shop. They *were* ready, and luckily Stacey had the BSC treasury with her, so we paid for them with the money the kids' parents had given us. (They'd all been happy to donate a few dollars to our project.)

We spent the rest of the afternoon back at Charlotte's house, looking over the pictures (there were some *terrific* ones) and talking about how to put together the book for Dawn. Suddenly the project was really starting to take shape, and we were all pretty excited about it. That afternoon, I forgot about the mystery at the bank, and so did Stacey and the kids. The mystery was still just that—a total mystery. It was *much* more fun to think about our project.

7th CHAPTER

"Look at *this* one," said Jessi, with a giggle. "Can you believe the face Jordan's making? You'd think he was having a tooth pulled out at the dentist's, instead of just having a trim at the barber's."

"He *hates* haircuts," Mal said. "Always has. That picture says it all."

My friends and I were gathered in my room on Monday afternoon, and our BSC meeting was just about to start. While we waited for Kristy to call the meeting to order, we listened to the radio and leafed through the pictures the kids had taken during our *Day in the Life of Stoneybrook*. There were so many good ones! It was going to be hard to decide which ones to include in our album.

Oh, there were a few disasters, of course. Vanessa had taken a whole series of pictures featuring a giant thumb, for example. Mal

65

explained that Vanessa would spend ten minutes setting up a "perfect" shot, and then forget to keep her fingers out of the way at the last minute. And Buddy's roll included several completely black frames— he'd forgotten to take off his lens cap for those. Charlotte had a habit of chopping people's heads off when she photographed them, and Becca wasn't too sure how to focus.

But still, it was amazing how many wonderful pictures there were. The whole series of the triplets' haircuts, for example. And Suzi's shot of a beautiful, glowing bride. There was Jamie's picture of Bart and Kristy at the ballfield, and Nicky's close-up of Pow's nose. Matt and Haley had taken some great pictures at their picnic, of a crowd of kids signing a mile a minute. And Charlotte's shots of the window of Polly's Fine Candy were so good they could make your mouth water.

In fact, seeing those pictures made me crave chocolate, so I went on a frantic search for a bag of chocolate hearts I'd hidden two weeks ago. At last I found them, tucked into a box of pastels. As the clock clicked over to five-twenty-nine, I helped myself to a couple of hearts and tossed the bag to Jessi. Then I reached over to turn the radio off, as I knew Kristy was about to start the meeting.

"Leave it on," Kristy said.

"What?" I asked. I couldn't believe my ears.

"Leave it on," she repeated. "Who knows? We might hear some more news about the bank."

"There wasn't anything in the paper yesterday," said Mal. "I checked."

"So did I," said Stacey. "All the police said was 'no new leads'. I don't know if they're *ever* going to solve that case."

"Order," said Kristy. "We can talk about the bank mystery later. First we have club business to take care of." She turned to Stacey and raised her eyebrows.

"Right," said Stacey. "It *is* subs day." She grinned and held up the manila envelope.

We all groaned and rolled our eyes. We like to give Stacey a hard time about collecting subs. She passed the envelope around, and we dropped our subs money into it. Then the phone started ringing, and we set to work lining up jobs. Stacey got one with Jamie and Lucy Newton, Mal and Jessi were booked to sit for the Pike kids, and I took a job with the Barretts.

Kristy had just hung up the phone after arranging the job with Mrs Barrett when we heard the "beep-a-deep-deep" that news stations use to introduce a special bulletin. Kristy and I both reached for the radio's

67

volume control, almost clunking heads as we dived for it. I grabbed it first, and turned it right up.

"Stoneybrook police, working in conjunction with security officers at the Stoneybrook Bank, have announced a lead in the bank robbery case," said the announcer.

We leaned forward and listened as hard as we could. This was exciting!

"According to videotape records, the disappearance of large amounts of cash could only have taken place between the hours of one and four p.m. on the Sunday before the cash was reported missing. During that time, the bank's video cameras were disabled and no footage exists. Police are speculating that the crime might have been an 'inside job'."

The announcer went on, but by then we had stopped listening. Instead, we were sitting there open-mouthed. "Oh, my *lord*," I whispered.

"Can you *believe* it?" asked Mary Anne.

"It can't be true!" said Shannon. "Do you realize what this means?"

"It means," said Mallory slowly, "that the robbery really *did* happen while you lot," she looked at me and Mary Anne, "were there taking pictures."

"This is just too amazing," said Jessi.

"Claudia, where are those pictures?"

asked Kristy, sounding very serious. "Get them out!"

I jumped up and pulled open one of my desk drawers. As slobby as I am usually, I can be very neat when it comes to certain things. My negatives are stored carefully in a three-ring notebook, with the contact sheet for each set tucked into a plastic envelope. They're all in order, and they're all dated. I even have notes about exposure times and film types. I found the contact sheet with the bank pictures on it right away. Then I took out my eyeglass and began to look through the pictures.

"Let *me* see," said Kristy, after I'd looked for a few seconds. I passed her the eyeglass and the contact print, and she scanned the pictures. Then, one by one, all my friends looked them over. When everybody had taken a turn, we sat quietly for a minute, thinking.

"It *has* to be the man in the suit," said Mal.

"Definitely," I agreed. "Just what I was thinking."

"He works at the bank," said Shannon, "so he'd know how to turn off the security cameras."

"And he was near the bank on Sunday afternoon," finished Jessi triumphantly.

"And I bet he wasn't just outside it, either," said Mary Anne. "I bet he went in. Look how he was dressed, in that dark suit."

"Even though it was a hot, summer day!" said Kristy. "He *must* have been planning to go into the bank. Maybe he was pretending to do some work there."

"And the police *said* it was an inside job!" I added, suddenly remembering.

"Guilty, guilty, guilty!" said Stacey. I gave her the high-five.

"Just one moment, girls!"

We turned to see who had spoken. It was Janine, who was leaning against the door-frame, looking into my room. "I couldn't help overhearing your conversation," she said. "And I must point out that there are some serious deficiencies in your reasoning. Most, if not all, of your evidence is purely and unequivocally circumstantial."

"Excuse me?" I asked. As I've said, there are times when what Janine is saying goes straight over my head. I mean, I knew what *some* of those words meant—even the big ones, like "circumstantial". I've done detective work before, and that word has come up. But when she strings a whole lot of big words together like that, sometimes I lose track.

"I think what Janine means," said Shannon, "is that we haven't really got any hard evidence. Just because that man was near the bank on Sunday afternoon, doesn't mean he's a criminal."

"That's true," said Mary Anne. "After all, he could have been wearing a suit because he was going to church."

"Exactly," said Janine, nodding at Mary Anne.

"But what about 'gut feelings'?" I asked. "What about hunches? I've got a *definite* hunch about this guy."

"Intuition has been established as having a place in criminal procedures," Janine said, nodding. "However, in no way can it substitute for authentic and valid evidence that can be presented to the judge and jury."

Whoops! She'd lost me again. But I didn't care. A hunch was a hunch, and suddenly I had a strong one. Strong enough to make me want to follow it up.

"Hey, Mary Anne," I said, as soon as Janine had left the doorway. "Did you write down that special number they gave out over the radio last week? The one you're supposed to call if you have any information or tips on the bank robbery?"

She checked her notebook. "It's right here," she said, tearing out a piece of paper and handing it to me. "But you're not really going to *call*, are you, Claud? I mean, we're not sure of anything."

"Oh, you're being too cautious," I said.

"After all, they didn't say to call if you had *proof*. They said to call if you had tips or information. And that's what we have." I grabbed the phone and dialled. When a man answered, I spilled out the whole story, starting with, "You see, my friends and I were making this book—well, not really a book, but an album—for another friend of ours. Her name's Dawn, and she lives in California. Well, she doesn't actually *live* there. . . Anyway," I went on, noticing that Kristy was giving me the "hurry up" sign, "we took these pictures, and they all show this man in a dark suit, and. . ." I went on and on. I suppose I was a bit nervous. The man on the other end just listened. Eventually I finished. "So, what do you think?" I asked him.

"I think this is a particularly *un*funny prank phone call, and I'm asking you now not to tie up this line again, young lady." He rang off before I could say another word. I stared at the receiver, shocked.

My friends were shocked, too, when I told them what had happened. "That's not *fair*," said Jessi.

"She's right," said Kristy. "And here's what I think we should do next."

On Tuesday, as soon as my classes were over, we put Kristy's plan into action. After Monday's meeting, I had printed up a set of pictures, each one showing the man in the dark suit. I took them down to the police station, where Kristy and Stacey were waiting for me. We went in together. This time, we decided we'd tell our story with illustrations. I showed the pictures to the officer behind the desk, while Kristy explained why we thought they might be important evidence.

"Nice pictures," said the officer, waving them away. "But I'm afraid they wouldn't mean much in court. Why don't you—"

"Hold on there, Sauter." A tall police sergeant with black hair and clear blue eyes had just come up to the desk. I'd seen him before, when we'd talked to the police about other mysteries the BSC had been looking into. I couldn't remember his name, though. "These girls have been helpful before, you know," he said. Then he turned to me. "Let's see those photos." I handed them over, and he looked at them carefully. Then he shook his head. "I'm sorry, girls," he said, "but I think Sauter's right. This man may just live near the bank, and there's nothing illegal about taking a stroll on a Sunday afternoon. These pictures probably *would* be classed as circumstantial evidence. We'll follow up the lead, but it doesn't look too promising. If you come up with anything else, let me know. Just ask for Sergeant Johnson if you call or come in."

And that was that. But as we walked out of the police station, I realized that, like it or not, we really were involved in this mystery now. "Okay," I said to my friends, "so the pictures don't prove anything. All that means is that we have to find some more evidence. Some *better* evidence. Then they'll believe us." Suddenly I was sure that if we tried hard enough, we would crack this case.

"So, what do we do next?" asked Stacey. We'd just left the police station, and were now sprawled on a couple of park benches outside the civic centre. It was hot by then, and the sun was directly overhead. I was trying to sit on the little patch of my bench that was in the shade.

"Good question," said Kristy. "But I haven't got an answer. Seems to me we're stuck."

"I know," I said. "It's frustrating."

The three of us sat silently for a few minutes, just thinking. As I've mentioned, we *have* done a little detective work in the past. I tried to think over some of the other cases we've solved, just to get some ideas. But you know what? Every case is so different. What works on one case may not be right for another. This case was *really* special too, because we had those

75

photographs. I felt rather like a private detective, this time. You know, one of those guys in a trench coat who lurks in dark alleyways, keeping his camera ready just in case Mr Criminal shows his face.

Waiting and watching. Those seem to be the two things that all detectives need to be good at. I thought about that for a second, and suddenly I had it. "A stake-out!" I cried.

My friends jumped. "What did you say?" asked Kristy.

"Let's stake out the bank," I said. "Maybe, just maybe, if we watch closely enough, we might find some more clues. Maybe we can even prove that the guy in the suit was involved in the robbery."

"Great idea," said Kristy, frowning a little. I think she's always just a little disappointed when somebody *else* has great ideas. She likes to be the one to come up with them.

"When should we do it?" I asked.

"How about right now?" Stacey said, jumping to her feet.

"Why not?" asked Kristy. "As Watson always says, 'there's no time like the present.' You know what, though? I think we should call Shannon. I know she'd want to help out. Too bad Jessi and Mal and Mary Anne are all on sitting jobs. They'd probably like to come, too."

"It's just as well," I said. "We don't want to have *too* big a crowd. If we were all there, it might look rather suspicious."

We headed for the bank, stopping on the way to phone Shannon and tell her to meet us there. As we walked, we argued about the best way to handle a stake-out. Well, maybe *argued* is too strong a word. But we did disagree. Kristy thought we should station ourselves behind the bank's columns and take notes on every single person who went into or out of the bank. Me? I thought that sounded like too much work. I thought we should just hang around opposite the bank, act like ordinary teenagers (whatever *that* means), and watch to see if anything suspicious happened.

Stacey sort of agreed with me, except she thought we could be a *little* more organized. "Maybe one of us should be *inside* the bank," she said. "And the others could each be paying attention to different things. One person could watch people going *in*, and somebody else could watch people going out. And maybe we could also watch to see if anybody's hanging around near the bank."

"Other than us 'ordinary teenagers'?" Kristy asked, teasing.

When we reached the bank, Shannon waved to us from across the street. We crossed to join her and filled her in on our plans. "How about if I go into the bank?" she suggested. "I've been thinking about opening a savings account there, anyway. I can ask about it today, and that'll give me a reason to be in there."

"Sounds okay to me," I said. The others agreed, too. So Shannon crossed the street again, and disappeared inside the bank, while the rest of us took up our positions. Kristy leaned against a pillarbox while Stacey and I stood nearby, trying hard to look casual. We chatted about our project for Dawn, and about our clients and how their summers were going. Meanwhile, all three of us were keeping a close eye on the bank. People walked in and out of the building, but none of them looked at all suspicious.

Then, suddenly, Stacey's eyes lit up. "Hey! Look who's about to go in." She started to wave. "Hi, Lo—" she began to call, but Kristy grabbed her arm.

"Shh!" she said. "Don't give us away. Besides, who knows? Logan could be a suspect."

"Are you mad?" I asked. "That's Logan Bruno. Mary Anne's boyfriend. Our friend. Associate member of the BSC. How could *he* be a suspect?"

"*Everybody's* a suspect," said Kristy. "And speaking of suspects, look who else is about to go into the bank." She pointed to the revolving door.

"Officer *Sauter*?" I asked. "But he's a policeman."

"You never know," said Kristy darkly. "Haven't you ever seen headlines about crooked policemen?"

We kept a close eye on the doors, and soon enough both Logan and Officer Sauter walked out, looking completely innocent. If either one of them was the criminal, it was clear that he hadn't engineered a bank robbery *that* day. Personally, I thought Kristy was mad. Logan and Officer Sauter, like everyone else going into and out of the bank, were probably just there to make deposits or check their balances. For a minute, I wondered whether this stake-out idea was really worth it, after all.

"Aha!" Kristy said, just then. She held up a finger.

"What?" I asked.

Kristy just nodded, looking mysterious.

"*What?*" asked Stacey. "Have you just worked something out?"

"I certainly have," said Kristy. "I worked out where that delicious pizza smell is coming from." She pointed down the road, to Pizza Express. "I'm *starving*," she said.

"Me, too," I said. "Maybe we should go

and get Shannon and find something to eat."

"Hey, look," said Stacey, nudging me. "Isn't that the woman from the pictures? The one with the pram?"

I turned to see. The woman was on the other side of the street, just down the road from the bank's main doors. "Yes, it sure is," I said. "And if we're going to pick up Shannon anyway, maybe we can take a closer look at her."

We crossed the street, keeping the pram in sight. The woman pushing it was a young mother, with curly red hair and loads of freckles. She pushed the pram along, leaning down now and then to coo the baby and rearrange its blankets.

I smiled at her as we neared the pram. "Nice day for a walk," I said, trying to lean towards the pram and see the baby.

"Isn't it?" she asked, turning the pram to the right so that I couldn't see a thing.

"How old is your baby?" asked Stacey, trying to peep over the front of the pram.

"Just two months," said the woman, turning the pram to the left.

"Girl or boy?" asked Kristy.

"Girl," said the woman. Then she wheeled the pram away briskly.

"Hmmm," said Kristy, as we watched her walk away. "*That* was suspicious. I wonder why she didn't want us to see the baby."

"Maybe there *isn't* a baby," I said thoughtfully. "Maybe the pram is actually full of money bags."

"That's rather far-fetched," said Stacey. "But who knows? Stranger things have happened." We all watched as the woman disappeared round a corner. Just as we lost sight of her, Shannon *flew* out of the bank's front door.

"He's the vice-chairman!" she said.

"Who? What?" I asked.

"That man in the pictures," she said. "The one in the suit. I've been watching him. He's vice-chairman of the bank."

"He *is*?" I asked. "Hmm. . ."

"I found out his name, too," she said, "but come on. He's going to lunch, and we've got to follow him." She pulled us behind the pillar, and we all watched as the man in the suit walked out of the bank and down the street.

"It looks as if he's wearing the same suit," said Stacey under her breath, as we followed him along the pavement. "And he's definitely wearing that watch, again, too."

"His name's Mr Zibreski," whispered Shannon. "I saw his name tag."

"And right now," I said, "Mr Zibreski's going into that coffee shop." I watched as he disappeared into Thelma's Cafe.

"Well, what are we waiting for?" asked Kristy, as we paused outside. "Let's go in. I mean, we're hungry too, right?"

We looked at each other, shrugged, and went in. I'd never been to Thelma's before, but it seemed like a nice enough place, with turquoise leather booths and waiters and waitresses wearing turquoise-and-white uniforms. Kristy headed straight for the booth behind the one Mr Zibreski had chosen. Stacey and I exchanged a panicked look, but we followed her, and so did Shannon. Just as we'd sat down, a man in a navy-blue suit approached Mr Zibreski's booth and Mr Zibreski stood up. "Frank!" he said, sticking out his hand for a shake. "Good to see you. How's Lillian?"

"She's fine. Says to send her regards to Gretchen," said the man. "Been waiting long, Jim?"

Jim! His first name was Jim. Already we were learning things.

"No, no, just arrived," said Mr Zibreski. "Sit down, sit down."

The two men sat down and started to look at menus. We were looking at *our* menus, too. "Mmm," said Kristy. "Cheeseburger deluxe. That's for me."

I tried to look at the menu and listen to the men's conversation at the same time, but it was hard. Eventually I gave up and concentrated on the menu until I found the perfect thing: a toasted cheese sandwich with bacon and tomato. I put my menu aside and looked over at Mr Zibreski's booth, which Kristy and I were facing. Shannon and Stacey had their backs to Frank and Mr Zibreski, but I could see that they were straining to hear everything the men said.

The waitress stopped at their booth first, and Mr Zibreski ordered a steak sandwich. Frank asked for the low-calorie dish: a hamburger patty and cottage cheese. (Ugh!) Then she came to our booth, and we ordered. After that, we started listening hard. We must have looked rather odd: a booth full of people who weren't speaking to each other. But Mr Zibreski and Frank didn't seem to notice.

"Bad news about that robbery," said Frank. I saw Shannon's eyebrows shoot up.

Mr Zibreski waved a hand carelessly. "The police are on the case," he said. "It'll be taken care of."

I thought that was interesting. He was either *pretending* not to be upset about it, or he really *wasn't* upset. Either way, it could mean something. We listened for more talk about the robbery, but unfortunately there was none.

The four of us sat quietly, munching our food (Stacey had a tuna sandwich and Shannon was eating a BLT) and listening to every word Frank and Mr Zibreski exchanged. And let me tell you something: it was about the most boring conversation I have ever heard. First they talked about mortgage rates. Then they talked about golf. After that they discussed the new sewer tax. Pretty soon I noticed that Kristy was yawning and Stacey was checking her nail varnish. I finished my sandwich and asked the waitress for our bill.

"I thought detective work was supposed to be *exciting*," I said, as we left the cafe. Nancy *Drew* always overhears good stuff when she tails suspects." The others cracked up.

"At least we got a good lunch out of it," said Kristy. "But next time, I hope he goes to Pizza Express. I've still got a craving for pizza."

We all went home after that, feeling rather let down. We'd spent the whole afternoon playing detective, and the mystery at the bank was no closer to being solved. I was definitely going to keep an eye on the woman with the baby *and* Mr Zibreski. But if we didn't come up with a few more clues—*soon*—we were never going to crack the case.

9th CHAPTER

On Tuesday, I spent the whole day thinking about the bank robbery case. But on Wednesday, by the time I was walking home from summer school, I had forgotten all about it. Instead, I was thinking about my photography class, and about Mr Geist.

Let me say straight away that I haven't got a crush on Mr Geist. Well, okay, maybe I have got a *little* one. I admit that he's quite cute, for an old guy. He's got black curly hair and these cool-looking wire-rimmed glasses, and he's tall and lanky. He's got a great smile, too.

But my feelings about him were more complicated than just a crush. Have you ever had a teacher who really inspired you? A teacher who seemed to believe you were capable of doing anything you put your mind to? A teacher who encouraged you, and made you want to prove that you could

85

do great things? Well, I'd never had a teacher like that before, but now I did. Mr Geist was definitely the best teacher I'd ever had, and more than anything, I wanted to please him. That day in class he'd explained some more about portrait photography, and he'd said some really inspiring things. He also showed us some really cool printing techniques that could help make good pictures great.

During class, I realized that I'd been so caught up in the bank mystery—and with our *Day in the Life of Stoneybrook* project— that I'd put my portrait assignment on hold. But I had the feeling those quick shots I'd taken of my friends might really be the beginning of a terrific project. One that would bring that great smile to Mr Geist's face. Suddenly, I couldn't wait to close my darkroom door behind me and pick up where I'd left off with those pictures. The negatives had looked good, I remembered, but I wanted to work hard on making perfect prints from them. And after that day's class, I had some new ideas about special techniques I could use.

The house was empty when I arrived. Janine was at her work-study job, and she'd said at breakfast that she wasn't planning to be home until dinnertime. And my parents were at work, of course. I had a quick lunch (a microwave tortilla—the closest thing to junk food I could find in the kitchen) and went upstairs to change.

That day I'd worn one of my favourite outfits to school: a lacy white shirt with big ruffled sleeves over a deep green leotard, with a short denim skirt and my favourite shoes (at least my favourites *that* summer): big black clunky boots.

Since I knew I was going to be in the darkroom, I threw off all my good clothes and pulled on a pair of shorts and my ancient green Sea City T-shirt. I piled my school clothes on a chair, promising myself that I'd hang them up later. Then I sat down at my desk and pulled my negative file out of the drawer.

I leafed through the contact prints, looking for the one with the portraits of my friends on it. When I got to the one with the bank photos, I paused. I picked up my eyeglass, thinking that one more quick look wouldn't hurt. There was Mr Zibreski, strolling up and down in front of the bank. And there was the lady with the pram. I examined each picture carefully, but no new clues showed up. It was frustrating.

"If only I had more pictures," I said out loud. After all, I still didn't know exactly when the crime had taken place. What if it had happened right *after*—or right before—I'd taken those photos? I might have actually captured something on film.

Then, suddenly, I thought of something. "Whoa!" I said, shoving the negative file back into the drawer. I jumped up and got my camera bag out of the wardrobe. I unzipped it with shaking hands and pulled out my camera. It was just as I'd thought.

There was still a roll of film in the camera. The roll I'd worked part-way through when I was in town with the kids. The roll I'd been shooting when Buddy and Charlotte pulled me away. More pictures of the bank!

There were still ten frames left on the roll, but I didn't care. Quickly, I rewound the film and popped it out of the camera. I had totally forgotten about my portrait project. This roll of film had pushed everything else out of my mind.

I grabbed my radio and went into the bathroom, remembering once more that I hadn't got around to making that *Darkroom in Use* sign. But I didn't stop to worry about it, as I knew no one else would be home for hours. I pulled the door close behind me and shoved a towel into the crack. When I turned on the radio, Billy Blue was singing "It's All Right", which I thought was a good sign.

Then I got to work. Quickly, I arranged my equipment. I set up the film reel and made sure I was all ready to load the undeveloped film on to it. Giving the counter one last look, I snapped off the lights and began to load the film on to the reel. It didn't take me long. As I wound the reel, I thought about what I might find when I developed the film. Would there be incriminating evidence? Would I be able to march into the police station and show them pictures that *proved*, beyond the shadow of a doubt, that a certain person was guilty? My heart was beating fast as I imagined how impressed the police would be.

Once all the film was on the roll, I reached for the developing tank. In a few more seconds, I'd be able to turn on the lights. I groped around on the counter, trying to find the tank, but it wasn't where it should have been. "Darn!" I said, realizing that I must have been in too much of a hurry when I arranged everything. I felt around a bit more, and at last I found the tank and its lid. I was just about to slip the reel of film into the tank when a horrible thing happened.

Somebody opened the door.

I gave a little yelp. "Hey!" I said, looking up at the door. The light from the hall filled the bathroom, blinding me for a few seconds. I saw a dark shape at the door, but there was no way to tell who it was. And whoever it was didn't say a word. Then, before I knew it, the door slammed shut and I was back in the dark again, with little white spots dancing in front of my eyes.

"Who's there?" I yelled. There was no answer. I sat there in the dark for a second, holding the reel of film. Then I dumped it into the tank and screwed the lid on. I would still develop it, just in case there were a few pictures that weren't completely ruined. As soon as the film was in the tank, I reached up and turned on the lights. Then I opened the bathroom door and peered out.

"Anybody there?" I called. "Janine? Mum? Dad?" There was no answer. Suddenly, I felt a chill. Who had opened the door? And where was that person now? I had thought I was alone in the house.

I headed into my room and—I know this will sound silly—looked under my bed. There was nothing there but the usual mess. Then I tiptoed to my bedroom door and peered out on to the landing. It was empty and silent. I checked Janine's room, and my parents'. After that, I took a deep breath, went downstairs, and checked the whole house. Nobody was at home; that was obvious. And the funny thing was that both the front and the back doors were locked! If somebody *had* come in, *how* they had got in?

The whole thing gave me the creeps.

I went to the kitchen, poured myself a glass of orange juice, and guzzled it down. Then I picked up the phone and rang Stacey. "Stace," I said, when she answered. "Something weird's just happened. Would you mind coming over to keep me company?

While I waited for Stacey, I went back upstairs to the darkroom and, with the lights on and the door ajar, began to develop the film. Soon I was so involved in watching temperatures and timing that I nearly jumped out of my skin when I heard a loud banging coming from downstairs.

"What? What is it?" I yelled.

"It's me!" A faint voice drifted up from outside. Stacey's voice. "The door's locked."

I ran down to let Stacey in. "Phew!" I said. "I'm feeling rather jumpy." I filled her in on what had happened and asked her to come up and sit with me while I finished developing the film. She perched on the edge of the bath and watched while I went through the final steps. When I'd finished, I hung up the film to dry and we both had a good look at it. Every picture was covered with a cloud of grey.

"Nothing," I said. "It's completely ruined. Now we'll never know what was on it."

Stacey tried to cheer me up, but nothing she said really made me feel any better. And when the rest of our friends turned up for the BSC meeting, and we explained what had happened, none of *them* made me feel better, either. In fact, something Mallory said after the meeting was over made me feel much, much worse.

"Maybe it was Mr Zibreski who opened the door," she said. "Maybe he *is* the guilty person, and maybe he knew you had those pictures."

"Ooooh, creepy!" said Jessi. "I bet you're right."

"You mean you think I'm being *followed*?" I said, with a shudder.

"Maybe we're *all* being *followed*," said Kristy darkly.

"Maybe Mr Zibreski is the head of a big gang," said Mary Anne, looking terrified. "Who *knows* what they'll do next?"

"Hold on, hold on," said Shannon. "I think we're getting a little carried away. A *gang*?"

"It could be true," said Stacey. "Anyway, even if it wasn't a whole gang, somebody *did* open that door. Who was it?"

We all exchanged panicked glances. Just a few hours earlier, I had been sitting in the dark, feeling secure in the knowledge that I was at home alone. But I *wasn't* alone.

Somebody else was in the house. And he wasn't a member of my family, I was sure of that. If he had been, he would have answered when I called out, and I would have found him when I searched the house. No, it had definitely been an outsider. The question was, *why* had someone opened the darkroom door? Was it just out of curiosity, or did he have a purpose? Was he out to ruin my film and make sure I couldn't prove what I hoped to prove? And how had he got in and out when the front door was locked? Maybe he was a professional.

My head was spinning.

"I'm just so sorry you lost that film," said Mary Anne. "You must feel terrible about that. Now we only have those other pictures, the first ones. And we can't tell anything from those. If only I hadn't made fun of you for taking pictures of the bank, we might have a lot more." She sat with her face in her hands, looking glum. Then, suddenly, she sat up straight. "You know," she said slowly, "I've just thought of something! There *are* more pictures of the bank, and they're still in my camera." She turned to me. "Remember? While I was using that one roll of black-and-white film you gave me, I took a whole lot of pictures of *you* taking pictures of the bank, just for a laugh." She got to her feet. "I'm going to ride home and get them right this second," she said.

"Great!" I said. "And I'll develop them the minute you get back. Or, on second thoughts," I added, thinking of the stranger on the other side of my bathroom door, "maybe I'll wait till my parents get back."

10th
CHAPTER

Of course, by the time Mary Anne got back with the film, my parents *were* back from work, and so was Janine. Mary Anne handed me the film and said she couldn't stay because her dad and Sharon wanted her home for dinner. "But I'm *dying* to know what you find out," she said. "Call me!"

I was on my way upstairs, thinking I'd go straight into the darkroom, when my mum called from the kitchen. "Claudia, time for dinner," she said.

"Oh, Mum," I said, walking into the kitchen. "I'm really not hungry, and I've got some work to do in the darkroom. Can't I skip dinner, just this once?"

She shook her head. "You know how I feel about that," she said. "Dinnertime is just about the only time our family is all together. I'd like you to sit down with us so we can all talk."

"Okay," I said. "Do you want me to lay the table?" I was hoping I could at least hurry dinnertime along, if I had to be there for it. I grabbed the plates, table napkins and cutlery and threw them down on the dining room table, laying it in record time. Then I went back into the kitchen and helped my mum put together a salad to go with chilli con carne my dad had made.

At last, after what seemed like hours, we were all sitting down at the table. As usual, my parents asked Janine and me how our days had gone. "Fine," I said, trying to keep it short.

"I had a wonderful day," said Janine. "I worked at the lab straight through lunch, and Professor Woodley said my research techniques were excellent." I thought she gave me a strange look when she said she'd worked straight through lunch, but I ignored it. I had a feeling I knew what she was thinking: that I was a real lightweight because I sometimes complained about having to go to school till midday every day during the summer. Well, I didn't care *what* she thought. If she wanted to be a work-aholic, that was fine with me. As long as she didn't expect me to be the same.

I bolted my chilli con carne, ploughed through a small plate of salad, and asked to be excused.

"No dessert?" my dad asked, pretending to be in shock.

"It's blueberry pie," said mum, trying to tempt me.

"I'll have some later," I said. "Just this moment I need to develop some film. By the way, Janine, that reminds me. I still haven't made a sign for the darkroom, so could you please just knock before you open the door?"

"Of course," she said. "Destroying your film once was enough. I'll take every precaution to avoid repeating the error."

"Er, all right," I said. "Thanks." Sometimes I wonder about Janine. She's brainy, no doubt about it. But will she ever learn to talk like an ordinary person? I jumped up from the table, took my plate into the kitchen and rinsed it, and went upstairs.

For the second time in one day, I went through my film-developing routine. I brought my radio into the darkroom, and I stuffed the towel under the door. I set up my chemicals and equipment, and this time I checked everything twice to make sure the tank would be where I could find it. Then I switched out the lights and began to load Mary Anne's film on to a reel.

About ten minutes later, I switched the lights back on and gazed happily at the closed tank sitting on the counter. Mission accomplished. Now all I had to do was develop the film. That routine is second nature to me by now, and I went through it easily, singing along to the radio as I worked.

Without going into too much detail, here's how film developing works. The tank, which doesn't let any light in, has a small hole in the centre of the lid. That hole leads to a little tube that goes down into the tank, so you can pour chemicals in and out without any light getting in. So. First, you pour developer into the tank, and start the timer. You tap the tank a couple of times to get rid of air bubbles. While the film is developing, you have to "agitate" the tank (that means move it around) every so often. Then, when the timer rings, you pour out the developer and straight away you put in this stuff called stop bath, which (duh) *stops* the developing. You agitate that for a little while—only about thirty seconds—and pour it out. Then you pour in the fixer, which makes the images on the negative permanent, and helps to harden the negative. The fixer stays in for about five minutes, and you agitate the tank once in a while. And finally, you pour out the fixer and, while the film is still in the tank, rinse the film (my dad helped me attach a little hose to the water tap). Once that's done, you put in a wetting agent to help keep water spots off the film. Then you take the film out of the tank and hang it up to dry. That's all there is to it!

As soon as I pulled the film out of the tank I could see that Mary Anne's pictures had come out very well. The images were clear and the contrast (the difference between blacks and whites) was good. But before I could make a contact sheet and take a closer look, I had to wait for the negatives to dry.

I cleaned up my equipment and put everything away, still singing along to the radio. Then I unplugged the radio and brought it back into my room, so I could listen to it while I did my maths homework. I sat down at my desk, pulled out my negative file, and took a longing glance at the contact sheet of my portrait series. I still wanted to work on that project, but it would have to wait. When I'm involved in a mystery, it's hard for me to think about anything else until the mystery is solved.

A few hours later—*long* after my mum had popped in to tell me it was time for bed—I sneaked back into the darkroom and checked to see if the film was dry. It was, so I made a contact print as quickly and as quietly as I could. Then I went straight to bed. I was totally exhausted, and I knew there was no point in looking through Mary

Anne's pictures until I'd had a good night's sleep.

I woke up early the next morning and sat right down at my desk with the contact print and my eyeglass. Here's what I saw: first there were a whole lot of shots of Buddy, Suzi, Charlotte and Becca fooling around. There were also a few pictures of the kids *taking* pictures. With a red grease pencil, I circled some of the best shots, thinking they'd look great in Dawn's album.

Then, at last, I found what I'd been looking for. The pictures of me taking pictures of the bank. Mary Anne must have thought I looked pretty funny, because she took quite a few pictures: me, squatting to frame a low shot; me, squinting as I focused; me, turning the camera practically upside-down to snap a shot of the carvings next to one of the pillars. But guess what? None of the shots showed anything suspicious at all. Mr Zibreski was in a couple of them, but he wasn't doing anything different from what he'd been doing in the other pictures. Same for the lady with the pram.

I put down my eyeglass and sighed. No new clues. Not one.

"Claudia!" called my mother from downstairs. "Time to get going!"

"Coming!" I called. But I couldn't resist. I picked up the eyeglass and took one more look. Then I saw something. Something important. In three of the pictures, where I was standing alone in front of the bank, there were windows behind me. And one of the windows looked different from the others. I squinted and screwed my eye into the eyeglass for a better look. It was unmistakable! One of the windows was lit up.

I sat back and thought. Why would one of the rooms in the bank be lit up—on a *Sunday*, when the bank was closed? Of course, it was *possible* that somebody had left the light on accidentally. But it seemed much more likely to me that somebody had been *inside* the bank at the time those pictures were taken. Somebody who was involved in the bank robbery.

"Cláudia!" my mum called again.

"I'll be right down," I yelled. Then I reached for the phone and called Mary Anne.

"Hello?" she said sleepily.

"Mary Anne, it's me, Claud. I think I've found a clue in one of your pictures."

"Really?" She sounded alert now.

"Can you meet me at the bank at one o'clock?" I asked. "I'll go down there straight after school. I'll bring the pictures for you to see. There's something I want to check out."

"I'll be there," said Mary Anne.

When I'd rung off, I grabbed a few things from my desk: the contact sheet, the eyeglass and a packet of loose change I'd been meaning to bring down to the bank. I threw them into my rucksack and went downstairs for breakfast.

At one o'clock sharp, I met Mary Anne in front of the bank. "Look at this," I said, showing her the contact sheet.

"What is it?" she asked. "I can't see anything funny. Unless you count that picture of Buddy making a face."

I pointed to the three pictures I'd found that morning. "See how this window is lit up?" I asked.

"Whoa!" she said. "What do you think it means?"

"I don't know for sure," I said. I turned to look at the bank. "We'll have to go inside to work out which room that window is in. I've brought this loose change, so we've got an excuse to go in." I started towards the main door of the bank.

"Hold on," whispered Mary Anne, grabbing my arm. "Look!"

I followed her gaze, and saw the woman with the pram walking towards us. "It's her!" I hissed. "Let's make sure to get a look at that so-called baby this time."

We walked towards the pram, smiling. But the woman turned it sharply and pushed it past us. I thought quickly. Could I distract her for a minute—just long enough to check under that yellow blanket inside the pram?

Suddenly, I threw my bag of loose change on to the ground, and it split open, spilling all the coins.

"Oh, no!" cried Mary Anne.

"Oh, dear!" cried the woman with the pram. She and Mary Anne bent to pick up the coins. Quickly, I stepped forward and reached into the pram. I flipped down the blanket and looked inside.

There was a baby in there.

A cute, red-haired, smiling baby, dressed in a little white sleepsuit with blue stars and moons all over it. As I gazed at the baby, the mother straightened up and glared at me. "Adorable baby," I said sheepishly.

The woman covered the baby up again and strode off, pushing the pram quickly.

"Protective mum!" I said to Mary Anne, shrugging. "At least we know she's innocent, though."

"You're right," said Mary Anne. "And that means—"

"That means Mr Zibreski *must* be the thief!" I said, knowing as I said it that my reasoning was full of holes. "He's our only suspect now," I continued, trying to convince myself. I glanced at the bank, checking that window again. Just then, I saw somebody staring *out* of the window, looking straight at me.

"Oh. My Lord." I said, under my breath.

It was Mr Zibreski himself.

"Mary Anne!" I said. "He's staring straight at us! Wait! Don't panic! Just act normal!" I felt frozen into place.

"Let's get out of here!" said Mary Anne. She tugged at my arm.

We ran all the way home, looking over our shoulders at every corner. I was sure I saw him behind us a couple of times. For the rest of that afternoon I watched out of my windows, sure that Mr Zibreski had followed us. Detective work had always seemed fun, before. This time, it seemed dangerous. This time, we were mixed up with somebody who was stalking *us* while we were stalking him.

11th CHAPTER

"Sergeant Johnson, please." It was the next day, Friday, and Mary Anne, Stacey and I were standing in front of the main desk at the police station.

The night before, Mary Anne had called me and we'd had a long talk. She was really worried about my safety, if there was "even a possibility" that Mr Zibreski was following me. "I think we should go to the police again," she said. "Remember, Sergeant Johnson said to let him know if we found out anything more."

"But we still haven't any *proof*," I said.

"I know," she answered. "But he might be interested in those pictures that show a light on in the bank. And it just seems to me that it couldn't hurt to have the police kind of keeping an eye on you—on *us*. Know what I mean?"

Mary Anne had been pretty convincing, so as soon as I'd finished at summer school the next day, I met her and Stacey in front of the police station. Of course, I'd brought the most recent pictures with me. (I'd made enlargements of the most interesting ones.) We marched straight in.

"I'll see if he's here," said the officer at the desk. It was a woman this time. She punched a button on the intercom, and spoke into the phone in a whisper, looking at us over her glasses as she talked. I had a feeling she was wondering what business three teenage girls would have with Sergeant Johnson. When she finished speaking, she listened for a second, and then, looking surprised, she hung up. "He says he'll be right out," she told us. "Please have a seat."

The three of us crowded on to a bench. While we waited, I dug the pictures out of my rucksack. I flipped through them again, and my heart sank a little. Sergeant Johnson probably wouldn't think much of them as evidence.

"What can I do for you girls?" Sergeant Johnson was standing in front of us, smiling.

I gulped. "You said to come back if we had any new evidence," I said. "Well, I don't know if these are evidence or not . . ." I held out the pictures, and Sergeant

Johnson took them and leafed through them. "You see, there's this light on in the window," I said, standing up and pointing to the picture he was looking at. "And the same man is in some of these shots. We found out that his name is Mr Zi—"

"Why don't we go somewhere else to talk," Sergeant Johnson said abruptly, handing the pictures back to me. "Somewhere a little more private." He led us past the desk, telling the woman officer, "We'll be using interview room four."

The three of us exchanged glances as we followed Sergeant Johnson down the corridor. We passed a room full of police officers working at typewriters, and a water fountain where some other officers were standing around, talking. Then Sergeant Johnson unlocked a door and ushered us into a small, quiet room which was empty except for a big table with several chairs around it.

I looked around the room. It looked just like one of those rooms in the films, the ones in which the police question suspects. Sergeant Johnson closed the door behind us, and the noise made me jump a little. Suddenly, I felt my heart beating fast. Were *we* under suspicion, for some reason? Was Sergeant Johnson going to start interrogating us? I looked over at Mary Anne and noticed that she had gone very, very pale.

Stacey seemed to be keeping it together, but I could tell she was nervous by the way she was twirling a lock of hair around her finger.

"Sit down, sit down," said Sergeant Johnson. "Make yourselves comfortable."

That was rather hard to do, as the room wasn't exactly the cosiest place I'd ever seen. We each pulled out one of the scruffy-looking orange plastic chairs and sat down, but I noticed none of us relaxed. I, for one, was sitting on the edge of my seat. We sat along one side of the table, and Sergeant Johnson took a seat on the other side.

Sergeant Johnson looked across at us, and he must have seen how tense we were. "It's okay, I'm not going to bite," he said. "Now, let's see those pictures again." I pushed them across the table. Picking each one up in turn, he examined them closely.

"Very interesting," he said, nodding. He scribbled some notes in a little notebook and then slapped it shut. "Now, what were you going to say about Mr Zibreski?" he asked me. He looked at me intently with those clear blue eyes.

"Just that we're still wondering about him, as he shows up in so many of the pictures," I said hesitantly.

"We *were* also wondering about the lady with the pram," Mary Anne added, her voice just a little shaky, "but now we're pretty sure she's innocent."

Sergeant Johnson smiled. "You're probably right about that," he said. "As for your friend Mr Zibreski, well—" He leaned closer and lowered his voice. "He *is* under investigation." He leaned back.

"He *is*?" I asked.

Sergeant Johnson nodded. "This is just between us, understand?"

We all bobbed our heads and said, "Yes *sir*!"

"We haven't really got anything on him," said Sergeant Johnson, "but we're suspicious, just like you. We searched all the employees' offices, including his, but we didn't find a thing. Then he gave us an alibi that didn't check out with what your *other* photos proved about his being at the bank on Sunday. So we searched his flat too. Nothing there, either." Sergeant Johnson scratched his head. "Zibreski's been completely cooperative, but somehow we think there's something fishy about him. But there's no sign of any irregularities in his banking accounts. What we really need is a picture of him *carrying* something out of the bank that afternoon. A suitcase, for example. Something he could have put all that money into. You haven't got anything like that, have you?"

I thought for a minute and shook my head.

"Without that," said Sergeant Johnson, frowning, "and without a definite time frame for the pictures you took, we really can't prove a thing."

Time frame. Time frame. My thoughts were racing. "We'll keep trying to find something," I said.

"Good, good," he said, standing up. I stood up, too, and so did Mary Anne and Stacey. I realized that our little meeting had ended.

Sergeant Johnson saw us to the door and sent us off with a pleasant goodbye. It seemed as though we had a real friend at the police station, and that was reassuring. But as soon as we walked out of the building, I started to feel nervous again about Mr Zibreski. I looked all around, wondering if he had followed us, and if he knew we were talking to the police about him. Mary Anne and Stacey were glancing over their shoulders too, so I knew they were thinking the same thing.

"Maybe he really *is* dangerous," said Mary Anne, and I knew she was talking about Mr Zibreski. "I'd feel safer if we were back at your house, Claud."

We raced back to my house, convinced, once again, that Mr Zibreski was at our heels. I was still thinking over what Sergeant Johnson had said about needing a time frame, and by the time we all pounded up the stairs to my room I'd had an idea. I threw Mary Anne's pictures down on my desk and then pulled out all the other bank pictures and added them to the pile. "Let's look at these again, and see what we can find in each of them that might help us to tell the time."

"Huh?" asked Stacey.

"I know what she means," said Mary Anne. "Like, if there's a clock in the background or something," she explained to Stacey, showing her a picture that featured a clock.

"Or if the shadows are falling a certain way," said Stacey, catching on. She picked up another print and showed it to us. "See? This one must have been taken later than the one Mary Anne's holding."

"Exactly!" I said. "So, let's put them all in order." We settled down to work, spreading out the pictures on the floor and sorting them into piles. Some of them showed the clock. Some showed the lighted window. Some showed Mr Zibreski walking towards the bank, and others showed him moving away from it. And lots of them showed the woman with the pram, who walked up and down in front of the bank, sat down on a bench for a few shots, and then seemed to leave the area.

Eventually, we had them arranged in an order that made sense to us. Then I took the pile, straightened the pictures, and flipped through them.

"It's like a film!" squealed Mary Anne.

"Do it again," said Stacey, eagerly.

I flipped through the pictures again, a little slower this time. As they weren't all taken from the same spot it wasn't *exactly* like a flip book, but you could definitely get an idea of the action. We watched as Mr Zibreski appeared from the right crossed paths with the woman with the pram, and disappeared. The light in the bank's window went on while the woman with the pram paraded in front of the bank, sat down on the bench, and then vanished. Then the light in the window went off, and Mr Zibreski reappeared and headed to the left. The clock that showed in some of the pictures kept track of the time throughout the whole thing. "Whoa!" said Stacey.

"Whoa is right," I said. "This is great!"

"It looks as if Mr Zibreski goes into the bank, turns on that light, stays a while, and then leaves," said Mary Anne, breathlessly. "This is *proof*!" She paused. "Isn't it?"

"Well, no," I admitted. "It's not proof that he robbed the bank. But it does seem to prove that he went inside that day, between one o'clock and one-thirty."

"That doesn't necessarily mean any-thing," said Stacey. "He could just be a workaholic, like my dad."

We flipped through the pictures about a hundred more times. Then we did it again, for the other members of the BSC. (They arrived for our meeting to find the three of us still sitting on the floor.) Everybody was pretty impressed by what we'd done, but we agreed that there was no point in going back to Sergeant Johnson, as the pictures *still* didn't show Mr Zibreski carrying anything. If he'd really stolen that money, he would have had to carry it out of the bank, after all. The bank had been thoroughly searched, and the money wasn't inside.

"You'd better hide those," said Jessi at one point, gesturing at the pictures. "I mean, what if Mr Zibreski really is follow-ing you? He'd love to get his hands on them."

Later that night, as I prepared to go to bed, I kept replaying Jessi's comment in my mind. At first I tried to convince myself that there was no way that Mr Zibreski could really be after me, but the more I thought about it, the more scared I became.

Here's what I did before I went to bed. First, I hid the pictures under my least favourite clothes (my gym uniform!) in my bottom drawer. Then I rigged up my own,

113

patent-pending super-alert burglar alarm. I ran strings from my bed to the door of my room, and I tied old film canisters all along them so that they'd jangle if they were touched. Then I propped an old suitcase full of books against the door, so that it would make a loud thump if it was knocked over. I put a jar full of marbles next to the suitcase, so that if the suitcase fell over it would knock the marbles all over the floor and make walking impossible.

Guess what? The alarm worked perfectly! But it wasn't Mr Zibreski who set it off.

It was me.

I got up to go to the toilet in the middle of the night and walked straight into every one of my own traps. First I stubbed my toe—hard!—on the suitcase, and a second later I was slipping and sliding all over the room on those marbles, while the film cans jangled away. I must have looked pretty funny. One day maybe I'll laugh about it. One day, when the bruises have disappeared!

12th CHAPTER

Saturday

What a job! Putting together this book for Dawn was like trying to launch a space shuttle or something. Or maybe more like trying to put on a big Broadway play. It's just that there were all these details to take care of, and all these *people who had opinions about how to do things, and — augh! But you know what? I think it's going to be very, very worthwhile. Dawn's going to be crazy about this book.*

Does Jessi sound frustrated and overwhelmed in that note of hers from the club notebook? Well, that's because she was. And with good reason.

I missed out on most of the chaos, because I was at home swotting up for an *extremely* important maths test that was scheduled for Monday. It was going to count for a large part of my grade, and if I didn't pass it I had the feeling my parents would never let me touch a camera again. They were already beginning to suspect that my photography course was much, much more important to me than my maths class. They were right, of course, but I had to show them that I could still pass maths.

Anyway, here's the scene: most of the people involved in the *Day in the Life of Stoneybrook* project were gathered at Mary Anne's house, around her big dining room table. Jessi had brought Charlotte and Becca over, along with Buddy and Suzi Barrett. Kristy had come with Jamie Newton, and also Matt and Haley Braddock. And Mal had brought Vanessa and Nicky.

The Spier-Schafer dining room table was crowded, to say the least.

And it was covered—*covered*—with mounds of pictures. Every photo we'd taken that Sunday was sitting on that table, and there was no room left for anything else. Jessi took one look at the pile of photos and the crowd of kids, and, as she told me later, "I wanted to turn and run out of the room." She had a feeling, right from the start, that it wasn't going to be easy to sort out that mess.

"Dawn's going to *love* these!" said Nicky, holding up a handful of pictures of the triplets having their hair cut. "We'll have to put all of them in the book."

"No way!" said Suzi. "If we put all those in, we won't have room for these other good ones." She waved a handful of pictures at Nicky.

Charlotte and Becca were giggling and shrieking as they looked through the

117

pictures of themselves with "moose ears" and "rabbit ears". Jamie was looking over their shoulders and jumping up and down as he giggled, too.

Matt Braddock was signing enthusiastically to Mary Anne, who kept shaking her head and signing, "Whoa, slow down, Matt."

Haley interrupted. "He says these pictures we took of the picnic are the best ones, and they should be in the front of the book. And I agree with him. Ours are the only pictures that don't have thumbs in them, and none of them are out of focus."

"Hey, what are you trying to say?" asked Buddy. "Are you telling me that our pictures are no good?" He looked at the picnic shots. "And anyway, why would Dawn want to see a whole lot of pictures of kids she doesn't even *know*?"

Haley started to translate for Matt, and then gave up when he started to look angry. She folded her arms and just sat there, glowering at Buddy.

Jessi exchanged glances with the other sitters. "Okay," she said, speaking loudly so she could be heard over the din, "let's calm down for a second. We've got a lot of work to do here—"

"And we won't be able to do it if we're fighting," finished Kristy.

"Do you lot want to make this book or not?" asked Mal.

"Think how much Dawn will love it, if we ever finish it," put in Mary Anne.

"We *know*!" said Suzi. "But it has to be fair. We have to decide how we're going to do it."

"That's right," said Jessi. "So let's start *talking*, instead of arguing. Okay?"

"*I* think we should put the pictures in chrontological order," said Charlotte, very seriously.

"Chrontological?" asked Buddy. "What the heck does *that* mean?"

"I think Charlotte means *chronological* order," said Jessi. "Like, in the order you took them. Starting with the first ones, and going on from there. Not a bad idea, Char," she added, "in fact, I think that's the way *A Day in the Life of America* is put together."

"But do we put the ones *I* took first?" asked Nicky. "Or the ones old Suzi-gooey took first?"

Suzi made a face. "Don't call me names, Nicky Pike," she said, putting her hands on her hips.

"All right, all right," said Kristy, frowning at both of them. "Here's another question. Should we write captions for the pictures, or just let them speak for themselves?"

"Captions would be nice," said Mary Anne.

"And I'll write them all!" said Vanessa. "They can be in rhyme, so the whole album will be like a wonderful, long poem." Ignoring the gagging noises Nicky started to make, she stared off into space dreamily, as if she were already beginning to compose.

"Hmm . . ." said Mal, looking rather doubtful. "Well, maybe not *every* picture needs a rhyming caption."

"What are we going to do about *this*?" Becca asked suddenly, picking up the photo album Mary Anne had bought to hold the pictures. "I mean, it's rather yucky-looking."

Mary Anne looked hurt for a second, but then she nodded. "You're right," she said. The album was powder-blue fake leather, with gold trim around the edges.

"We can make a cover for it," said Haley. "You know, with artwork and a title and all our names on it and everything."

"Like a real book!" said Jamie. "I've got *lots* of books. I can help make the cover!"

"You can't even write yet," Vanessa reminded him. "I've got the best hand-writing here," she added. "I can make the cover after I do the captions."

"You're not the boss!" screeched Jamie. He looked as if he were about to cry.

Suddenly, Jessi had had enough. "That's it!" she said, standing up and glaring around the table at everyone. "This is supposed to be a fun project. Let's stop fighting, and start working." While she was watching the others squabble, she'd had an idea. "Here's what I think we should do," she began. Quickly, she outlined her plan.

Ten minutes later, the scene in Mary Anne's dining room was very different. The kids had broken up into groups, and each group had a task. Mary Anne was supervising Haley, Buddy and Nicky, who were in charge of picking out which pictures should go into the book. They worked at the table without too much arguing, as Jessi had been clever enough to pick one person from each picture-taking group. Straight away they picked out a pile of "must-haves" to pass on to the others.

Becca and Charlotte sat at the other end of the table, working at putting the pictures into some kind of order, as Kristy offered occasional suggestions. Vanessa and Suzi made themselves comfortable at another section of the table, thinking up and writing captions for the pictures—with a little help from Mal. And Matt and Jamie spread out on the floor with all the art supplies Mary Anne could round up. They looked through the craft paper and glue, paints, crayons and bits of fabric and wool (all laid out on top of newspaper, of course), and started making a cover for the album. Jessi watched to make sure they didn't make *too* much of a mess.

At last, the project was under way. And an hour later, when Sharon (Mary Anne's stepmother and Dawn's mum, in case you forgot) poked her head into the dining room, she smiled and said, "You kids work so *well* together!"

The four BSC members glanced at each other and tried to hide their smiles. Sharon went on. "It's just wonderful that you're doing this for Dawn," she said. "She'll *adore* it. And as I told Mary Anne, I'll be glad to help by packing it up and posting it on Monday."

After we'd thanked her and she'd left, Mary Anne whispered to Jessi. "I'll make sure it actually gets to the post office. You know how she can be. That parcel might end up in the oven!" They both giggled. Dawn's mum is a bit absent-minded at times.

The work was going well—in fact, the album was almost finished—when the peaceful scene was broken by an argument between Nicky, Haley and Buddy. "There's only room for one more picture," said Haley.

"And this is it!" shouted Buddy. He

waved a picture of himself in his Krushers T-shirt, on first base.

"No way!" said Nicky. "What about this one where Adam's about to kick the barber?"

"Hey, you lot!" sighed Kristy. "You've been doing so well. Don't spoil it by fighting. How about if you let everybody else vote on it?"

The three of them agreed, and Kristy took a quick poll. Unfortunately, when the votes were counted up, the result was a tie.

"We need a tie-breaker. Phone somebody else and ask them!" said Buddy. "One of the other sitters. They'll know which is best."

And that's how I finished up taking a break from my studying. Stacey, Shannon and Logan were out, and I was the only BSC member left to call. I was happy to do the job, as the numbers on the pages of my maths book were beginning to run together by that time.

I popped over to Mary Anne's, and within seconds I'd done my job and broken the tie. (I picked Buddy's picture, as there were already about seven pictures of the triplets all ready to go into the album.) Then I sat down and started leafing through the rejected pictures, just to make sure the "selection committee" hadn't missed any of the ones *I* thought we should use.

Most of them were rejects for a good reason. All the thumb ones and all the completely black ones were in there, plus a few of those "missing-head" shots of Charlotte's. But then I came across a series of pictures that made me gasp with surprise. Without saying a word to anybody, I grabbed five or six of them and jumped up from the table. "I'm taking these," I told Jessi. "Gotta run!"

Jessi told me later that as she watched me head out of the door she *knew*, just *knew* that I'd found another clue to the mystery. But she could also see that I was in a big hurry, so she didn't stop me to ask questions. Instead, she turned back to helping the kids complete the album and compose a short letter to Dawn. She knew she'd be hearing about what I'd discovered soon enough, and meanwhile, there was a project to finish.

13th CHAPTER

Jessi was right. I *was* in a big hurry. I ran all the way home from Mary Anne's, clutching that handful of photos. Then I pounded upstairs to my room and sat down at my desk. I turned on the overhead lamp for better light, grabbed my eyeglass, and prepared to take a closer look.

Up until that afternoon, I was sure I'd seen every bank photo taken that Sunday. But now I was looking at pictures I hadn't seen before. These weren't pictures of the bank's façade, or even pictures of me taking *pictures* of the bank's façade. These were pictures of a different part of the bank, one I hadn't been thinking about before. The cashpoint. Actually, the pictures were *supposed* to be of Suzi. I think Buddy had taken them. Unfortunately, only Suzi's right shoulder had made it into the picture. But the cashpoint had been captured perfectly.

125

What's a cashpoint? It's one of those places where you can get cash by inserting your bank card into the machine, and then punching in your personal code number. And the cashpoint at the Stoneybrook Bank is around the corner from the main entrance, which is why I hadn't given it a thought. Before now, that is.

What had caught my eye, over at Mary Anne's, was that out of six pictures of the cashpoint, five featured one woman. I could tell she'd been standing at the machine for quite a while, because it always took Buddy a long time to set up and shoot each picture. That made me suspicious.

It usually only takes a couple of minutes to withdraw cash from those machines. I know because I've seen my mum do it plenty of times. Practically every time we're in town together she ends up making a stop there. "I don't know *where* the money goes," she always sighs. "Didn't I just take out some cash yesterday?" She inserts her card, punches in her number (it's my birthday, she once told me, even though it's supposed to be a secret), and waits, tapping her foot impatiently, until the machine spits out her fifty dollars.

I've always thought cashpoints were pretty cool, the way the money comes out just like magic.

Anyway, I bent to take a better look at the

photos, and what I saw made me take a deep breath. Each picture showed the woman pulling a wad of bank notes out of the cashpoint. Apparently, as she pulled out each wad of notes, she put them on the little shelf while she punched in more numbers, because once I arranged the pictures in order, I could see the pile on the shelf growing and growing. In the last picture, the pile of notes looked really, really thick.

I sat back and let out that deep breath in a big sigh. Suddenly, there was a new angle to the bank mystery.

What if that woman had somehow rigged the machine so that it would give her as much money as she wanted? (Usually, there's a limit to how much you can take out in one day. You also have to have the money in your account to begin with.) And if those bills were big ones, like hundreds, that meant she could have withdrawn thousands of dollars! That could mean that Mr Zibreski was innocent after all. Maybe he really was just a hard-working banker, and maybe my friends and I had been wasting our time investigating him. I picked up the eyeglass again and studied the woman more carefully, but it was hopeless. Her back was to the camera, and there was nothing unusual about the way she was dressed—in a jogging suit and running shoes—that

127

would help me identify her.

Suddenly, I felt as though I needed to show the pictures to somebody else. Somebody who could help me work out what they might mean, and what we should do about it. I grabbed the phone and dialled Mary Anne's number.

"Mary Anne, have you lot nearly finished?" I asked, without even saying hello first.

"Actually, we've just finished. Mal's on her way out of the door with Nicky and Vanessa, and Kristy and Jessi are about to walk the other kids home."

"Great!" I said. "Tell them that I want you all to come to my house as soon as you can. I've got big news."

"What?" asked Mary Anne, sounding excited. "Have you cracked the case?"

"Well, maybe," I said cautiously. "I think I've got some important information."

"We'll be there as soon as we can," she said.

Just as I was about to ring off, I thought of something. "Mary Anne!" I said. "Wait! Can you bring the finished album—*and* all the pictures that didn't go into it? I want to look at every photo one last time."

Mary Anne promised to bring every single picture, and we hung up. I went back to examining the photos on my desk. By the time my friends turned up, about fifteen minutes later, I'd convinced myself that the woman at the cashpoint was the real bank robber.

Kristy arrived first. "Mary Anne says you've found a new clue," she said. "That's great! What is it?"

I showed her the pictures, and explained my theory about how the woman must have rigged the machine.

"Or maybe somebody *else* rigged it," Kristy said thoughtfully. "There could be a gang at work here, you know."

"Rigged *what*?" asked Jessi, who had just come into the room. I explained all over again, showing her the pictures. Then Mary Anne and Mal arrived. By then I was tired of explaining, so I let Kristy do it.

They pored over the pictures, taking turns with the eyeglass until everybody had seen enough. "Did you bring the other pictures?" I asked Mary Anne.

"Right here," she said, showing me the shopping bag she'd lugged over.

"Let's dump them out and look through all of them," Kristy suggested. "Who knows what else we might have missed?"

We sat down on the floor with the pile of pictures and started to sort through them. "You know," said Kristy, while we were working, "I saw this article in the paper about people who were rigging cashpoints. I can't remember exactly what they did, though."

"I remember!" said Jessi. "It was really pretty ingenious. They put this fake cash-point into a shopping mall, and they rigged it so it would record the codes people punched in. Then the robbers just made up copies of the cards, went to *real* cashpoint machines, and withdrew the people's money by using their secret codes."

"Did they get away with it?" I asked. Even though I knew what they'd done was wrong, I couldn't help admiring how tricky they'd been.

"Nope, the police caught them," said Kristy. "I remember that part." She picked up a photo. "Hey, here's another picture of that woman, and in this one you can almost see her face!"

"I've found one, too," I said. "Let's start putting them in sequence. Just look at the pile of bank notes she's got in *this* picture!"

Mal studied the print. "Wow!" she said. "Just think, if every one of those notes really is a hundred-dollar note we're looking at a lot of money."

"A *ton* of money!" Kristy said. "This is it! I'm sure of it. It's the big break we've been looking for."

"All *right*!" I said. "I can't wait to show these pictures to Sergeant Johnson. He's not going to *believe* we cracked the case. We really have got proof this time." Mary Anne and I finished laying the photos out, in order.

"We did it!" sang Jessi and Mal. They jumped up and started to dance around the room. "We did it! We did it!"

"Ahem!" We stopped carrying on and looked up to see Janine, standing in the doorway with her arms crossed. "Once again, I couldn't help overhearing your conversation. I hate to be the one to tell you, but your deductions are based on invalid reasoning."

"*What?*" all four of us said at once.

"You have pictures of a woman removing numerous bank notes from the cashpoint, correct?" she asked. "And, judging from the dimensions of the piles she has accumulated, you think the pictures may show that she's responsible for the robbery?"

"That's right," I said, a little doubtfully. I was beginning to see that we'd got carried away, but I still wasn't sure where Janine was going with this.

"The largest denomination of bills in most cashpoints is twenty dollars," Janine said.

"So?" I asked. I *still* didn't get it.

Janine picked up one of the pictures. "So this pile she has couldn't be worth more than several hundred dollars. And even if she *was* able to over-ride the limit on withdrawals, it couldn't be more than a thousand," Janine said. "I'm sorry to ruin your case, but facts are facts." She put the picture down and folded her arms again.

"Oh," I said. "*Now* I get it." I blushed. We had definitely got more than a little carried away. At least I hadn't called Sergeant Johnson yet. That would have been pretty embarrassing.

"Cheer up," said Janine. "Your reasoning may have been flawed, but your persistence is admirable. Keep it up! You may still work it out."

"Thanks," said Kristy, looking pretty depressed.

"Yeah, thanks," echoed Mal.

"Claudia," said Janine, "aren't you supposed to be studying for that test?"

I nodded and glanced at my maths book. I'd been stuck in the middle of a hard problem before Mary Anne phoned me, and I wasn't too keen to go back to it.

"I'd be glad to help you," said Janine. "Let me know when you're ready." She left the doorway and went back to her room.

For a second, nobody spoke. I think we were too embarrassed.

"We should go," said Mary Anne finally. "We don't want you to fail that test."

"Sorry for the false alarm," I said.

"That's okay," said Kristy. "Hey, don't

132

you want to see the finished album before we go?" I could tell she was trying to cheer me up.

"Of course," I said. We sat down on my bed and looked at what they'd put together that day. You know what? It was *terrific*. And seeing it did cheer me up. The cover had this great drawing: a map of Stoneybrook, with all the familiar places— restaurants, the schools, our houses— drawn in. The title was written in a banner across the top, in what I recognized as Vanessa's best handwriting: *A Day in the Life of Stoneybrook—An Album for Dawn*.

And the pictures inside were perfect. There was something special about each one. "This is *bound* to make Dawn miss Stoneybrook so much that she'll hop on the next plane home," I said, closing the album. "You lot did a wonderful job."

My friends left after that, taking the album with them. And then Janine and I hit the books. She is *great* at helping me with my studying. By the time we'd read through three chapters, doing all the problems along the way, I felt prepared for my test. The only weird thing was that Janine seemed rather distracted. She was fidgety, and she wouldn't look me in the eye. I thought maybe she felt bad about having to break the news to us that our "proof" wasn't proof at all. Then again, maybe she was having boyfriend troubles. You never can tell with Janine. And anyway, I didn't have the energy to wonder about it. One mystery at a time is enough for me.

14th CHAPTER

On Sunday morning, I woke up early. And as I lay there in my bed, watching a branch wave in the breeze outside my window, I thought about a dream I'd been having just before I woke up. In the dream, I was in my darkroom. Only it wasn't my patched-together, tiny bathroom-darkroom. It was a super-cool professional darkroom with every possible piece of equipment, and plenty of room for everything. In the dream, I was working at this huge enlarger, printing a picture that was as big as one of my walls.

I don't know what the picture was *of*. I only know it was huge.

I smiled as I thought of it, wishing I really *could* print pictures that big. You'd really be able to see every detail if you blew up a photo like that.

Then, suddenly, I sat bolt upright in bed.

Every detail. That was it! If we really wanted to use our pictures to solve the mystery, we'd have to be able to see every single detail of those photos. And blowing them up was exactly what I had to do. Of course, I couldn't blow them up as big as the picture in my dream, because I didn't have the equipment for that. But I *could* blow up parts of every picture—the parts that mattered.

I jumped out of bed and threw on my dressing gown. Then I went downstairs and had a quick breakfast. The house was quiet, as nobody else in my family was up yet. After I'd stuck my cereal bowl into the sink, I ran back upstairs and changed into an old pair of jeans and my Sea City T-shirt. Then I sat down at my desk and grabbed a piece of cardboard. With my fattest, reddest magic marker, I printed *DARKROOM IN USE* across it, and then held it up to admire my handiwork. At last, I'd remembered to make that sign. It was important to put it up before Janine woke up and barged into the bathroom.

Then I did one last thing before heading into the darkroom. I rang Kristy. "I think I'm on to something," I said. "A whole new way to look at the pictures. And I may need help—or at least a few more pairs of eyes. Can you phone everybody else and ask them to come to our meeting early tomorrow?

Say, at two o'clock? If we work anything out, we'll want to have time to go the police station."

Kristy agreed to let everybody else know, but she sounded doubtful about my new idea. "We've been over those pictures every which way, Claud," she said, yawning. I'd woken her up. "But if you think we might find something new, I suppose it's worth a try."

After I hung up, I grabbed my negative files and went into the darkroom, taping up the sign on my way in. I arranged my equipment and got to work straightaway. I worked for hours, printing picture after picture. I made blown-up copies of every photo I could. (I could only do the black-and-white ones, of course.) Then, when the prints were nearly dry, I brought them out into my room and hung them up in long rows along the walls. I paced up and down, looking at each one. There was Mr Zibreski, walking in front of the bank. There was the lady with the pram. I examined each one closely.

My mother tapped on my door at one point to ask if I wanted some lunch, but I told her I was busy. I didn't feel hungry at all: I was too involved in my work.

But there was a problem. No matter how carefully I stared at the pictures, I *still* couldn't find any clues. I needed more detail. At one point, as I was pacing around the room, I nearly stumbled over my camera bag. And that's when I had my *next* big brainstorm.

I pulled out my camera, checked to make sure I had film, and started clicking away. What was I taking pictures of? Well, this might seem crazy, but I was taking pictures of the pictures. It was the only way to focus in on parts of the photos I thought might give us some clues. I put my camera very close to some of the photos and shot pictures of smaller areas *within* them. When I developed the film, I would be able to blow up those areas even bigger. It may sound complicated, but it was really simple.

As soon as I'd finished the roll, I rushed back into the darkroom to develop it. And by the time the film was finished, the day had flown by and my dad was calling me downstairs for supper. I tore myself away from the darkroom and tried to act normal while I ate with my family. Then, after supper, I forced myself to stay out of the darkroom and spend one last hour with my maths book. I hadn't forgotten about my test.

By one o'clock on Monday, I was back in the darkroom, the maths test behind me. (I was pretty sure I'd passed, thanks to Janine's help.) Quickly, I made prints from the new negatives, again blowing them up as much as I could. Then I hung *those* pictures underneath the pictures I'd hung up the day before. Now one whole wall in my room was totally covered with photographs.

I started to look them over, but I'd only examined two or three of them when my friends started to arrive. "Wow!" said Kristy, when she walked into my room and saw the display of photos. "You've been working hard."

"I suppose so," I admitted. I'd been totally obsessed with printing these pictures, so obsessed that it hadn't even seemed like work.

"Look at how much more you can see," said Stacey, gazing at a picture of the lady with the pram. "I can see the baby's foot in this one. It's poking out from under the blankets."

"How cute," said Mary Anne, sighing.

"I never noticed before that Mr Zibreski's got a little bald spot," said Mal, giggling.

"This is great," said Shannon, after she'd walked up and down the room and looked at each photo. "All the pictures are here, and they're all in order. And you've blown up each one to show the most important details. If we don't find any clues this time, there aren't any to be found."

"Well, that was my idea," I admitted. "I

was hoping we could take one last look, just to be sure we didn't miss anything the other times.

And that's exactly what we did. For the next fifteen minutes, there was total silence in my room as my friends and I pored over the pictures, hunting for a clue, any clue that might help us solve the mystery once and for all.

"What about the ring this woman is wearing?" Jessi asked at last. She was looking at a blown-up picture of the lady with the pram. "Is that some kind of secret symbol?"

Mal peered at it. "Oh, that's one of those Irish wedding rings," she said. "You know, two hands holding a heart. I think they're really pretty."

"But it's not a clue," said Jessi, shaking her head.

"Neither is the baby's blanket," said Mary Anne, "but I have to say that it's really lovely how somebody embroidered all those animals on it." She had her nose pressed up to one of the pictures.

"Let's be serious," said Kristy. "I mean, I think we really need to examine these pictures of Mr Zibreski. After all, Sergeant Johnson *did* say that he was under investigation." We clustered around the pictures of Mr Zibreski and concentrated on them. We looked closely at his pockets—

both the ones in his trousers and the ones in his jacket—to see if money could be hidden in them. We checked to see if he could be hiding money under his shirt, but he was too slim for that. We even peered at his eyes, to see if he had "that guilty look", as Stacey said.

Nothing.

Then, all of a sudden, I noticed something interesting. "Look," I said. "In this picture he's looking at his wristwatch. And in the next one, he's checking the bank clock, as if he wants to be sure he's got the right time."

"So?" asked Kristy. "What's wrong with that?"

"Why is he wearing a wristwatch, when he's carrying that big pocket watch?" I asked.

"Whoa!" said Stacey. "Good point." She bent to look at the picture more closely. "I always thought there was something interesting about that banker's watch he carries," she added.

"Interesting?" asked Jessi in a strange voice. "You could say that. Look at this, you lot," she went on. "The time on the pocket watch never changes, even when the time on the bank clock *does*. What could that mean?"

"That the pocket watch is a fake!" yelled Kristy.

"I bet he's hiding something inside it. Something to do with the robbery," said Shannon. "A—a microchip or something."

Suddenly, out of the blue, I remembered a conversation I'd had in the bank one day with Charlotte. "Or," I said, realizing that the case was about to fall together, "a key."

"A key?" asked Mary Anne.

"That's right," I said. "I'd bet anything that he's got a key in there. A key to the safe deposit box, where he's hidden the money he took. He must have known the police would search his desk and his flat, but he knew they'd never look inside his watch. That's probably why he was so cooperative—he thought he'd outsmarted the police!"

"Claudia!" Kristy said, looking at me admiringly. "You're a genius. That's it! What else could it be?"

"Let's take these pictures down to the police station right this minute," said Stacey, starting to pull them down off the walls. The rest of us helped, and within half an hour we were all sitting opposite Sergeant Johnson, in that same room with the same orange plastic chairs. Only this time, there was one big difference.

Mr Zibreski was in the room with us.

The police had been in the middle of questioning the banker one more time when we arrived. When we showed Sergeant Johnson the pictures, he nodded. "Very interesting," he said. "This might be the final piece of evidence. I'll take them in and show them to our suspect. I think this might lead to a confession!"

"If it does, we want to be there!" said Kristy, putting her hand over the pictures and looking stubborn.

Sergeant Johnson didn't look pleased, but he thought about it for a minute. Finally, he brought us into the room with Mr Zibreski and asked us to explain what we thought the pictures meant.

I was so nervous I thought I'd pass out. But I took a deep breath and started to explain how the pictures proved that the watch wasn't working. "You see?" I said, pointing to the pictures I'd laid out on the table. "The second hand on the clock is moving in *this* shot, and in *these*—five, six, seven . . ." Then I pointed to the part of the super-enlarged pictures showing Mr Zibreski's watch. "But the second hand on the watch just stays absolutely still." I looked up at Sergeant Johnson, and he gave me a little nod and a smile. "That's how we worked out that the watch doesn't work at all, and that there must be some other reason why he—" I looked at Mr Zibreski. "Why *you* were still carrying it."

Sergeant Johnson looked over at Mr

Zibreski, too. "May I see the watch?" he asked.

Mr Zibreski unhooked it from the chain and handed it over without a word. He looked terrified.

Sergeant Johnson prised open the back of the watch, and something fell out, making a jingling noise on the table. My friends and I leaned in for a closer look.

It was a key.

"All right, all right," said Mr Zibreski suddenly. His voice was gravelly, and sounded strained. "Is it a confession you want? Well, here it is. Check box 528. The money's all there."

"*All* of it?" Sergeant Johnson asked coolly. He never seemed to get excited. Personally, I was about to jump out of my chair, and I could tell my friends were too, but I knew we had to let Sergeant Johnson handle the situation his own way.

"All of it," said Mr Zibreski, sounding tired now. "I haven't spent a penny."

And that was that. A few minutes later, two police officers came in and led Mr Zibreski away. (I actually felt quite sorry for him—he looked *miserable*.) Sergeant Johnson thanked us and told us he'd be in touch, and we left the police station.

Out on the street, we let loose with all the excitement that we'd built up in that little room. We jumped around, screamed, and gave each other high fives. "He was clever, that Mr Zibreski," I crowed. "But he wasn't clever *enough*."

Hours later, when I finally went to bed, I slept better than I had in weeks. For the first night in what seemed like a long time, I didn't have to worry about Mr Zibreski being after me. The case was closed, and he wasn't going to be around for a long, long time.

15th CHAPTER

"'Clever Teens Find Key to Bank Mystery.' How about that? My daughter's famous," said my dad, peering over the newspaper at me the next morning, as I sat down to breakfast.

"I *love* that headline," said my mum, passing me the jam. "And the article's terrific. The police gave you girls practically all the credit for solving the case."

"I know," I said. "Isn't it great?"

"Well, it's great that it worked out," said my mother, frowning. "But I would have been worried if I'd known what you were up to. Playing detective can be dangerous."

"Oh, Mum," I said. "We were careful. All we did was work out clues from those pictures we took."

"Your detective reasoning, though flawed at times, proved fruitful in the end," said Janine. She helped herself to some toast. I noticed she still wasn't looking me in the eye.

"I suppose that photography class is really paying off," said my dad.

"It certainly is," I said. "But do you know what? We might have solved the case a lot sooner if some of my pictures hadn't been ruined."

"Ruined?" asked my dad. "How?"

Janine and my mum looked at me curiously.

"Oh, just a mistake I made," I said. There was no way I could tell the truth. My parents would never let me "play detective" again if they knew about what had *really* happened. I thought for a second about how scared I'd been that day when somebody opened the darkroom door, but I shrugged off the feeling. The main thing was Mr Zibreski had been caught, and now I was safe.

The article mentioned that Mr Zibreski had been squirrelling money away for some time. Apparently, he couldn't stop worrying about his "retirement years", and stole money so he could be sure he'd have plenty when he was older. Reading the article, I realized he was a very troubled person, and I was glad to know he'd be in prison for quite a while. I wouldn't have to worry about him following me, and he would get the help he needed.

After breakfast, I went upstairs to get ready for summer school. Just as I was putting on my earrings—a pair I'd made out of green beach glass—I heard a tentative knock on my door. "Claudia?" Janine called softly. "May I come in?"

"Of course!" I said, opening the door for her. "What's up?"

Janine came in and sat down on my bed. Instead of answering me, she stared at her hands.

"What *is* it, Janine?" I asked. "Is something wrong?"

"No," she said, finally. "Well, I mean, *yes*—but . . ."

"Janine!" I said. "Spit it out!"

"It's just that I—I have a confession to make," she said, after a long pause. She blushed and looked down at her hands again.

"A confession?" I asked. "About what? Have you robbed a bank, too?"

"No," she said, smiling a little. "But I did do something wrong, and then I compounded the error by refusing to admit it."

"Huh?" I asked.

"I should have told you this a long time ago," said Janine. She took a deep breath. "I was the one who opened your darkroom door that day."

"I knew that," I said. "Remember? You

apologized all over the place."

"No, not *that* day. The *second* time."

"Ohhh!" I said. At last I realized what she was trying to say. "That was *you*?" I asked. "I was *sure* it was Mr Zibreski, trying to ruin my film on purpose."

"That's what I *thought* you thought," she said. "That's why I wanted to confess. I was just so embarrassed before that I couldn't bear to tell you. After all, I'd ruined your film once, and that was bad enough. Doing it twice was ridiculous. So when I realized what I had done that day, I just ran out of the house. I couldn't face you."

"Janine, you are a wacko!" I said, laughing. Then I remembered the "burglar alarm" I'd set up—and set off!—that night and I started to laugh even harder. It was such a relief to know Janine had been the one who'd opened the door.

"So you're not angry?" asked Janine.

I was laughing too hard to answer her, but I managed to shake my head. Then she started to laugh, too.

About a week later, I was putting the finishing touches to a special display in my room when Stacey walked in. She was a little early for our BSC meeting.

"Claudia!" she said, looking around at the pictures I'd hung up. "These are *great*." She stepped closer to one of them. "Looks as if Mr Geist thought so, too." She was pointing to a big red A+ written on a Post-It note stuck to the side of the photo.

"He loved them," I admitted, feeling rather shy all of a sudden. I remembered the way he'd smiled when he told me how well I'd carried out the portrait assignment. That's what those pictures were: my portraits, which I'd finally finished and handed in. Now I had them back, and I couldn't wait for my friends to see them. I gazed around the room and saw the faces of the BSC looking back at me. There was Kristy, shooting me the peace sign, and Mary Anne, throwing her hands over her face, Stacey, striking a pose and looking totally cool, Shannon, looking serious and thoughtful. And there was Jessi, caught in mid-*plié*, and Mal, showing the camera her pile of books.

Just to make the show complete, I'd added snapshots of Dawn and Logan, so the entire BSC was up there on my walls. The picture of Dawn was one she'd sent us from California, and it showed her carrying a surfboard as she walked across a beautiful beach. And Logan's picture showed him in his track uniform, after a big race.

"This is so, so cool," said Kristy, who'd come in behind Stacey. "Can I have a copy of the one of me?"

"Of course," I said. And by the time the

rest of the club members had arrived and looked at the pictures, I had orders for copies of *all* of them, and I'd also promised to make up a set to send to Dawn. I was going to be busy in the darkroom that night, but I didn't care. I was proud of my work, and happy that my friends liked the pictures as much as they did.

"I did really well in my maths test, so my parents agreed to let me keep on taking photography classes when school starts this autumn," I told them. "Mr Geist says I'm one of his most promising students!"

"Yea, Claud!" said Stacey. "I think you deserve a big round of applause—not only for these pictures, and for passing maths, but for all the work you did on solving the bank mystery."

"Hear, hear!" said Kristy. She started to clap, and everybody else joined in.

I gave a little curtsy. "Thank you, thank you," I said. "And now, to celebrate—" I held up a huge box of marshmallows. "Marshmallows all round! And popcorn, too," I added, passing the bag to Stacey.

Once our meeting began, we were busy for a while taking phone calls and arranging jobs. Then, during a lull, Kristy said, "You know, I've been thinking about that lady with the pram. I'd like to track her down."

"*Why?*" I asked. "She's innocent. We know that for certain now."

"I know," said Kristy. "But she *does* have a baby, you know. She might need a sitter one of these days."

That's Kristy for you. She never stops thinking about business!

Just after our meeting ended that day, the phone rang once more. I grabbed it. "Hello?" I said.

"Is this the famous Girl Detective of Stoneybrook?" somebody asked.

"Dawn!" I said. "Did you get the newspaper clippings I sent you."

"I certainly did," she said. "Great work! And I got the book you lot made, too. It's *wonderful*. I can't tell you how much it made me miss Stoneybrook."

I talked to Dawn for a few minutes, and then I passed the phone around the room so she could talk to everybody else. Before she rang off, she told Mary Anne that she was writing a thank-you letter to the kids who had made the book.

Dawn's letter arrived a few days later, and here's what it said:

Dear Everybody,

Thank you so much for making *A Day in the Life of Stoneybrook* for me. I look through it every day, and think about the people and places in Connecticut that I miss so much. Not to mention the excitement I'm missing out on — like catching bank robbers! You know, California is a wonderful place, and I love being with my dad and Jeff, but I think my heart really belongs back in Stoneybrook. And I promise you it won't be long before my body's there, too!

Thanks again — and love,

Dawn

Look out for Mystery No 17

DAWN AND THE HALLOWEEN MYSTERY

"Where do you think he might be?" asked Jill, biting her thumbnail. She quit chewing her nails a while ago, but sometimes when she's nervous the habit comes back.

"He could be anywhere," Maggie answered. She was lying across Sunny's bed, hugging a stuffed crocodile (Sunny's childhood champion—his name is Captain) to her chest.

"She's right," said Sunny. She sat on the floor, toying with her hair. "After all, once he took off that clown mask, he'd look like anybody else."

"I—I think we should try to find him," I said suddenly, surprising everybody—including myself.

"What?" asked Sunny.

"I said we should find him," I repeated, more sure of myself this time. "I mean, I know what I'm doing when it comes to detective work. If we caught him, it wouldn't be the first time I helped to solve a crime."

"Aren't you scared, though?" asked Jill, looking at me with big eyes.

"Sure," I said, shrugging. "I'd be dumb *not* to be. The guy *does* have a gun. But I know how to be careful. And anyway, wouldn't it be great if we really did catch him?" I leaned forward. "Just think! The kids could go trick-or-treating after all, and they wouldn't have to spend the rest of their lives remembering the time some crook ruined their Halloween."

Maggie was nodding fast. "You're right, Dawn," she said. "You're absolutely right!"

"I agree," said Sunny. Her eyes were sparkling. "After all, how hard can it be? You saw the guy. There are plenty of clues, right?"

I didn't even have to stop to think. "Here's what we do," I said. "If we find out where the guy is, we immediately call the cops and let *them* take care of it. Okay?"

"Okay," said Jill, after a second's hesitation. "What do we do first?"

"Let me think about it," I said. "I'll figure out a plan."

"Let's work on the case as often as we can this week," said Sunny. "We don't have much time if we want to save Halloween for the kids."